The Soc

# INCREDIBLE
# STORIES

## THE BEGINNING OF THE END

# The Society of
# INCREDIBLE
# STORIES

## THE BEGINNING OF THE END

## MIKE OAKLEY

Illustrated by ANDY OAKLEY

DORMOUSE PUBLISHING

First published in 2020 by Dormouse Publishing

001

www.dormouse-publishing.com

DORMOUSE™
PUBLISHING

Contact us at contact@dormouse-publishing.com

For my wife, Immy, and our two daughters who have watched me sit typing away on a keyboard, muttering to myself, for many a long year.

And in these unprecedented times, I would like to dedicate this book to all the critical workers and NHS staff who have worked tirelessly to keep everybody safe during 2020.

*Thank yous!*

A big thank you goes to my sister-in-law, Helen, whose tireless dedication to editing this tale has transformed my creative musings into something wonderful. I cannot thank you enough.

I would also like to thank Andy, my brother, who has been my creative companion on this journey, supplying not just the fantastic artwork found in this book, but for helping shape the story and characters.

And finally thank you to Becky, Alice, Molly, Sophie and Mattie for reading the book and giving your invaluable feedback.

# PROLOGUE

## *A Journey to Nowhere*

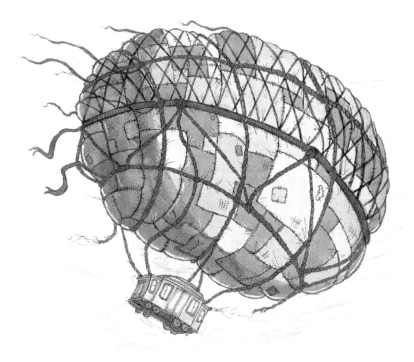

As the thick, grey clouds ebbed and flowed across a turbulent sky, a beaten old train carriage, attached to the underbelly of a large hot air balloon, gallantly fought back against The Storm.

On board, with her sturdy boots planted firmly on the polished floorboarded deck, Eliza Monroe stood before her airship's large wooden wheel and stared unflinchingly into the face of chaos. 'It's just you and me now, old girl,' she said, blowing a lock of hair out of her face.

She was well aware of The Storm's infamous reputation for devouring anyone daring, or crazy, enough to venture too close to its wall, but despite the seemingly impossible odds, nothing was going to stop her. She reached over and pulled on a brass lever, activating a pair of propellers outside. The sudden acceleration made every part of the carriage creak, crack and groan as the airship shot forward. As it thundered towards The Storm wall, Eliza knew that if she were to stand any chance of getting out alive, it wasn't just going to take every ounce of her physical strength, it would take an awful lot of courage and determination too.

Outside the carriage, the wind howled and screamed, and heavy rain hammered against the windows. As The Storm grew ever closer, Eliza felt her heart pounding in her chest and she gripped tightly onto the ship's wheel. 'Come on then, let's see what you've got. I dare you,' she said. As if replying to Eliza's taunt, a sudden and extraordinarily strong gust of wind blew out the carriage's front window, letting the chaos outside rush in. Eliza was instantly blown off her feet. Yet somehow, with her legs flapping freely behind her, she still managed to grip hold of the wheel.

'Like that is it?' she shouted, over the roar of the wind as the carriage veered violently to one side and then the other. The wind roared in her ears and plastered her now wet, curly hair across her determined face as her beloved carriage, the place she'd called home for most of her life, was being torn apart around her. Any other person would have given up at this point, letting the elements carry them away into the abyss, but not Eliza. She was a Monroe, and Monroes never, ever gave up.

'Is that the best you've got?' she cried. While still gripping onto the wheel, now with just one hand, she dug deep and managed to find the strength to reach over and pull on another brass lever beside her. An elaborate pulley system burst into life, and from the ceiling, a new window swung down to replace the one that was broken, blocking out the wind. Eliza instantly fell to the floor with a thud. Quickly, she scrambled back to her feet and stood behind the wheel again. 'Hah! Your move,' she retorted.

The mighty Storm continued to throw the carriage around, pulling it one way then jerking it the other, spinning it this way and that. All the while the ropes, that were just about holding everything together, continued to creak and groan. Eliza knew that they wouldn't take much more punishment before they finally gave out, and all she could now hope for was that the ropes would last just long enough to see her to safety. Eliza, wiped her brow with the back of her hand, adjusted her smoky goggles and wrapped both her hands around one last lever. 'Don't let me down now, old girl,' she said, taking a deep breath, before jerking the lever forwards.

A fork of lightning suddenly shot across the sky and hit the carriage. With an enormous bang and a shower of sparks, the airship vanished.

# CHAPTER 1
## *Eliza Monroe's Will*

Arthur Boil stared at the old grandfather clock in Mr Mumblecrust's office. Although the pendulum swung back and forth, he felt sure the mechanism inside it was broken. It was either that or time in the old solicitor's office really had ground to a halt. The reality was that Arthur had only been sat with his parents for little more than ten minutes, even though it seemed like hours.

'Look, can we please just get on with it?' said Arthur's father, breaking the silence as he finally lost patience with all the waiting around he was having to do, a thing that really did not come naturally to him. Unlike Arthur, who was content to sit quietly and wait, Mr Boil was more than happy to speak up whenever the occasion arose.

Mr Mumblecrust raised one bushy eyebrow and his thin purple lips pursed as he pointed a single bony finger at the grandfather clock. 'Proceedings shall begin in exactly ten minutes,' he said, placing his hands together on the desk in front of him.

'You what?' said Mr Boil, looking rather lost and annoyed.

'It means, Mr Boil, that when the big hand points up and the little hand…'

'All right, all right, I get it,' snapped back Mr Boil, but Arthur was quite sure he didn't. What Arthur's father made up for in brash confidence, he seriously lacked in intelligence.

Mr Boil groaned. 'This is blooming ridiculous, love,' he said to his wife, crossing his arms.

'What's ridiculous is that you can't sit still for two minutes,' snapped back Mrs Boil.

'Actually it's…' Mr Boil looked at the clock and went quiet as he silently counted his fingers. Finally, he replied, 'Nine minutes, and that's nine minutes too long. I'm bored, bored, bored.'

Arthur noticed the corner of Mr Mumblecrust's left eye twitch. 'Mr Boil, I have already stated on a number of occasions, we shall begin proceedings at exactly ten o'clock and not a moment before. So, may I suggest, you try and be a little more patient,' he said, picking off an imaginary piece of dirt from his perfectly clean desk.

Arthur could tell that it hadn't taken Mr Mumblecrust long to decide that Arthur and his parents were quite clearly from a much lower class than he was. The moment he saw them, his warm smile had instantly changed. The smile hadn't gone, that was still professionally fixed on his face, but Arthur could see his eyes had lost any flicker of warmth. He clearly hated having to deal with poor people, and they didn't come much poorer than the Boils. All Arthur and his parents had in the world were each other. The only reason they had a roof over their heads was that Arthur's Aunt Eliza had given them one.

Arthur looked over at his mother. She was a tall, sinewy woman, while her husband, the bombastic Mr Boil, was short, gruff and bristly. Arthur looked nothing like his father, but he did share a lot of striking similarities with his mother. Not only were they both tall and thin, they each had a mop of black, curly hair with a white streak running through it. A prominent feature that had also been shared by his Aunt Eliza. A sad realisation hit Arthur; they were all that was now left of the Boil family. Just two weeks earlier there had been four. Mrs Boil sniffed loudly and wiped a tear from the corner of her eye.

'You okay, mum?' Arthur asked.

'I'm fine, love. Just get a bit upset when I start thinking about my dear sister, that's all.'

Arthur went to his pocket and retrieved his handkerchief and passed it over to her. 'We don't even know that she's, you know...'

'Dead?' said Mr Boil, interrupting. 'She flew into The Storm, son.

There's no chance of her coming back from that. She'd have been smashed into a million pieces.'

Mrs Boil cried out in anguish.

'Dad!' said Arthur.

Mr Boil looked confused and it took him rather too long to realise his mistake. 'Oh right. Erm, sorry,' he said. 'What I meant to say was that she wouldn't have suffered too much. A mind can only function for so long when the body is being torn to pieces around it.'

Arthur put his face in his hands as Mrs Boil's nostrils flared. Before she could reply, Mr Boil turned to the solicitor. 'Look, Mr Crumblerust,' he said.

'It's pronounced "Mumblecrust".'

'Well, whatever you call yourself, we have clearly been sat for more than ten minutes. So, if you wouldn't mind, I'm supposed to be at a very important meeting at eleven o'clock.'

'Ha!' blurted out Mrs Boil.

'And what was that for?' said Mr Boil, turning to her.

'What meeting have you ever been to? You don't even have a job.'

'What are you talking about woman! I have my own business.'

'Don't you "woman" me, Gerald Boil. If you have your own business then how about you tell Mr Mumblecrust all about it,' she replied. 'I'm sure he'd love to know what it is you do exactly because I haven't the foggiest. I mean, isn't the idea of a business to make more money than you spend? Something you still haven't figured out yet.'

Mr Mumblecrust looked silently on as Arthur mouthed the words 'sorry' to him. Not that that did anything to remove the scowl now on Mr Mumblecrust's wrinkled, grey face.

'I have told you before that these things take time,' continued Mr Boil.

'And how many years have I been hearing that for? Twenty, twenty-five? Quite honestly, I've lost count. If it hadn't been for my dear sister, well, heaven knows where we'd be living now.'

Mr Boil sighed heavily. 'Not this again.'

'Yes, this again, Gerald,' snapped back Mrs Boil. 'Why can't you just get a normal job like everyone else? It's only because of my dear sister's generosity and kindness that we have never had to live on the streets and that she let us live with her in the train yard.' Mrs Boil choked on the last words. 'I'm sorry,' she said, dabbing her eyes. 'I just miss her so very much.'

'Me too mum,' said Arthur, patting her hand.

Mr Boil crossed his arms and grumbled something unsympathetic under his breath before Mr Mumblecrust finally found a moment to speak. 'Mr Boil, once more let me make this clear to you, the will shall be read at ten o'clock, and not a second earlier. Is that understood?'

Mr Boil huffed loudly, and, like a very impatient and very hairy

spoilt child, he went back to angrily swinging his short legs backwards and forwards under his chair.

After the few long minutes had passed, the grandfather clock finally chimed, and Mr Boil let out a great sigh of relief. 'At last! I thought I was going to die of boredom,' he said.

Mr Mumblecrust ignored the outburst and instead turned his attention to Mrs Boil. Arthur jumped as Mr Mumblecrust attempted a sympathetic expression which, to Arthur, looked rather terrifying. 'I read the story in the papers about your sister's… mishap, Mrs Boil. Most unfortunate,' he said.

Mrs Boil dabbed her nose with Arthur's handkerchief and just about managed to smile back.

'I understand that she was in possession of quite a bit of land?'

'You bet she was!' said Mr Boil, grinning.

Mrs Boil gave her husband a look that swiftly wiped the grin off his face. She then turned her attention back to Mr Mumblecrust. 'If you must know, yes,' she replied. 'The entire train yard belonged to her.'

'I see,' Mr Mumblecrust replied, and Arthur didn't like the way he said that one bit. The room fell silent. Mr Mumblecrust turned over the sealed envelope in front of him. 'Well, if we are all ready, I shall begin proceedings,' he said.

'About blooming time!' Mr Boil said, vigorously rubbing his hairy little hands together.

Again, that was a little too enthusiastic for Mrs Boil's liking and she shot her husband a look that froze his hands in place before he slowly put them back in his lap.

Mr Mumblecrust cleared his throat. 'Mrs Boil, I shall now read to you, in accordance with The Collective Law, the will concerning the estate of your sister, Miss Eliza Monroe,' he said, before opening the envelope in front of him with a small silver knife and removing the letter from within it. 'My dearest family,' he read, 'it is with a heavy heart that I have left this world for another.' Mrs Boil sniffed back tears. Mr Mumblecrust waited a moment before continuing, 'All I hope is you may all join me soon.' Mr Mumblecrust's eyebrows furrowed. 'I can assure you madam that I am only relaying to you what is written here in the will,' he said, holding up the letter to prove his point.

'Can't we just, you know, skip the boring part and get to the bit that matters, if you catch my drift?' said Mr Boil, winking at Mr Mumblecrust while rubbing his thumb and fingers together in the expectation there could be money coming his way.

'Dad!' hissed Arthur, gesturing to his mother.

Mrs Boil was staring at her husband with thunderous eyes and Mr Boil realised he was in trouble again. 'W-what I meant to say was, can't we go a little quicker since this is quite an upsetting day for my dear wife?' he said. Mrs Boil huffed loudly, making it quite clear she didn't believe a word of it.

'Mr Boil, I am legally bound to read the will out in full, every last word of it, and that is what I intend on doing,' said Mr Mumblecrust. 'I simply request you adopt an acceptable level of patience.'

'All right, all right, keep your bloomin' wig on Mr Crinklybust. It was only a suggestion.'

Arthur noted Mr Mumblecrust's left eye twitch again at that remark.

'Will you just shut up, you old fool, and let the man do his job,' said Mrs Boil.

Mr Boil huffed and crossed his arms. 'There's me only thinking of your feelings. That's really hurt me that has. Well you do what you like then and don't be surprised if I nod off.'

Composing himself the best he could, Mr Mumblecrust took a deep breath. 'If you have quite finished?' he said. Mr Mumblecrust shot Mr Boil a challenging look before looking down at the letter and continuing. 'I'm sure you are all wondering what will happen to my yard,' he read. Mr Mumblecrust licked his finger and slowly turned to the next page before carrying on, 'I spent a long time deciding who should actually inherit it. The one thing I am absolutely certain of is that it should go to one of my family. The last thing I want is for it to go to that pompous twit, Mr Mumblecrust.'

'Well really!' said Mr Mumblecrust, his face flushing with anger. Arthur stifled a laugh.

'I'm so sorry. I'm sure she didn't mean it. My sister was quite the joker,' said Mrs Boil, rather embarrassed.

'As long as she was a rich one, who cares?' replied Mr Boil, winking at Arthur.

Mrs Boil gave her husband yet another withering look before she turned back to the solicitor. 'Please try and ignore my husband, Mr Mumblecrust. Much to my constant embarrassment, he really is quite the most insufferable fool.'

'So, it seems,' he said under his breath, before he cleared his throat and continued. 'Here's the bit you've been waiting for, who gets what,' he read. Mr Boil, quite literally, sat on the edge of his seat. 'I leave all of my worldly possessions to my loyal friend, Trip,' said Mr Mumblecrust. Before he could continue, Mr Boil had jumped to his feet and was turning a worrying shade of purple. 'She's only gone and left everything to that blooming flea ridden cat,' he blurted out. He then started pacing the office, cursing some pretty ripe words under his breath.

'Mr Boil! Will you PLEASE sit down and moderate your passion!' said Mr Mumblecrust, now getting really rather angry.

Mr Boil was in no mood to take orders. 'She never did like me. Thought I wasn't good enough for her precious sister, she did.'

'You surprise me,' Mr Mumblecrust said through gritted teeth.

'I hated 'er in life and now I hates 'er in death too! Well, this is for you, Eliza!' Mr Boil looked up at the ceiling and blew a rather long and impressive raspberry.

'Gerald! Really!' Mrs Boil said, exasperatedly. 'That's my dear sister you're speaking ill of, you ruddy insensitive buffoon!'

'Well, Lily, dead or not, she deserved it!' he replied.

'MR BOIL!' said Mr Mumblecrust, the floodgates to his temper now fully open. 'SIT! DOWN! I won't ask you again.'

'Do as you are told, you stupid old fool! You're embarrassing the lot of us,' said Mrs Boil, looking over at Mr Mumblecrust with an ashamed expression on her face. 'I'm so sorry. He gets a little wound up at times,' she said.

Arthur was watching all of this with an amused smile on his face. It was true that Arthur's aunt didn't like his father. She'd told Arthur that his dad was always only ever interested in making money the easy way. 'Doing nothing, Arty, produces nothing,' she'd said to him on so many occasions he'd lost count.

Mr Boil grumbled and cursed under his breath, but he did finally do as he was told. Like a sulking child, with his bottom lip sticking out, he sat back down heavily in his chair and crossed his arms again.

After Mr Mumblecrust had taken a few long and rather deep breaths, he picked up the letter again. 'If you care to listen there is actually more,' he began.

'What's the point, she's given everything away,' said Mr Boil. 'We may as well go home, not that we have one to go to now.'

'Oh, will you just shut up Gerald,' said Mrs Boil before she turned to the solicitor. 'Please, do carry on Mr Mumblecrust.'

Mr Mumblecrust composed himself. 'Thank you,' he said, looking back down at the will and continued, 'I leave all of my worldly possessions to my loyal friend, Trip, AND to my wonderful, caring sister and her beaky nosed, money grabbing fool of a husband.'

Arthur's father couldn't believe his ears and he leapt to his feet crying out the most heartiest of 'hurrahs!'. He then did a merry jig around the office hopping from one foot to the other. 'Good old Eliza! Always liked the girl. God rest her soul,' he said with a great toothy grin on his face. 'We're rich! Rich! RICH!' he squealed, his voice getting higher and higher while he continued to dance around the room, giddy on his new-found wealth.

Mrs Boil, on the other hand, dabbed fresh tears away from her eyes and looked down into her lap. 'Unlike my foolish, cold-hearted husband, Mr Mumblecrust, I would happily trade everything just to spend one more day with my dear sister,' she said.

'Dad!' said Arthur.

Mr Boil realised he should probably have been a little more sensitive, and he sat back down. Now quite out of breath, he stretched over Arthur and patted his wife on the hand. 'There, there dearest, don't cry,' he said, grinning at her. 'Surely, this should be a day of celebration, no?'

Arthur looked on mortified as his father then went cross-eyed and tried to look at the generous protrusion sticking out of his face. 'Is my nose really that beaky, my love?'

'Yes, like a parrot's, you ruddy great buffoon!' she said.

Arthur stifled a laugh. The solicitor cleared his throat. 'If you care to listen, I haven't actually finished yet,' he said, now sounding like he wanted nothing more than to get the Boil family out of his office for good. Arthur and his parents looked at Mr Mumblecrust before he continued, 'To my beloved nephew, Arthur Tobias Montgomery Boil.' Arthur was taken aback to hear his name. 'I give to you this letter.' Mr Mumblecrust passed Arthur an envelope sealed firmly with a blob of red wax.

# CHAPTER 2

## *The Suitcase*

When Arthur Boil arrived home from the solicitor's office later that day, he couldn't get off the rickety old wooden cart quick enough. No sooner had Mr Boil brought the donkey to a stop, Arthur had jumped off. Before either Mr or Mrs Boil could stop him, he had run across the snow peppered yard towards the old converted train carriage they called home.

'Well, aren't you going to go after him, Gerald?' said Mrs Boil. 'Can't you see he's upset?'

'What? I think we should just let the lad be,' said Mr Boil.

Mrs Boil went quiet for a moment before reluctantly accepting that, on this rare occasion, her husband was probably right.

If truth be told, Arthur was glad to have some peace and quiet. During the journey home, his parents had done nothing but argue. No sooner had they left the solicitor's office and began the trek home, it had started. Mr Boil had turned to Mrs Boil with a grin on his face. 'So, how is my wonderfully beautiful wife feeling?' he said, placing a hand on hers. Ordinarily, this would have been a lovely gesture if it had been given by almost anyone else, but this was Mr Boil. Slowly, Mrs Boil had turned to face him, her eyes narrowing.

Arthur was well aware his parents had been married long enough for his mother to know when his father was up to his old tricks. Although they loved one another, Arthur's mother didn't completely trust her husband.

'Why?' she said, moving her hand away from his and crossing her arms.

'What do you mean, why? Can't a caring husband not even ask his wife how she is nowadays?' he said.

'Well, if you must know I am worried about what's going to happen to us now that Eliza isn't with us anymore,' she said.

Mr Boil looked down for a second before he turned to face Mrs Boil. 'Well, it just so happens I've been thinking about that,' he said, and a smile broke out across his face.

'Please tell me it's not another one of your hare-brained schemes,' she said.

'How dare you! I'll have you know that there's nothing hare-brained about my exciting business opportunities, thank you very much,' replied Mr Boil, sounding quite offended. 'You know you used to believe in me once.'

'Yes, once upon a time, when I was young and naive. We may

now own the train yard, but we still have bills to pay and they can't be paid with flights of fancy. You just need to get yourself a proper job like everyone else. Is that too much to ask?'

Mr Boil looked down at the tatty reins he held in his hands and then over to the tired looking donkey at the end of them. 'But I don't know how to do anything else,' he said.

'Well, you're going to have to learn then, aren't you?'

Mr Boil crossed his arms. 'Well, maybe I don't want to.'

'Well, maybe you don't have a choice.'

All had then gone quiet as Arthur sat at the back of the rickety old cart and said nothing, feeling the tension between his parents in front of him. He knew from experience that an argument between them was best left that way.

Mr Boil decided to break the silence. 'You know if we sold the yard, it would give us enough money to really get one of my business ventures up and running,' he said. 'It must be worth a considerable amount.'

Mrs Boil's nostrils flared, and her lips puckered, and Mr Boil instantly realised he'd crossed an uncrossable line. 'And there it is!' she shouted.

Mr Boil did a terrible impression of someone looking shocked and confused by throwing up his arms. 'What?' he said.

'Don't you "what" me, Gerald Boil. I should have known you were up to something.'

'Don't get your bloomers in a twist, love. It was just an idea.'

'And let me make this absolutely clear to you, you can forget it. We are not selling our home and that's that. You really are a sneaky so-and-so, Gerald, do you know that?'

'I was merely…' began Mr Boil before Mrs Boil stopped him.

'Just don't,' Mrs Boil said. 'I'm fed up with your constant scheming. You just can't bring yourself to do the right thing, can you?'

The argument had then continued the rest of the way home.

Arthur could still hear them bickering outside as he made his way through the little living room, and then the even tinier kitchen, before he finally reached the back of the carriage. There he climbed up the narrow wooden ladder to where his bedroom was. No sooner had he gone inside and closed the hatch behind him, Trip, his aunt's cat, and the reason for Arthur's father's embarrassing outburst earlier, sauntered over to him and rubbed his matted furry body against Arthur's legs. 'Hey Trip,' he said, tickling him behind his ears. Arthur then sat himself down on his bed and carefully broke the wax sealing the mysterious envelope. Inside it was a letter. He quickly removed it as Trip jumped up onto Arthur's bed and dropped himself down next to him.

Arthur opened up the letter and began to read:

*Dearest Arty,*

*If you are reading this then the wheels are finally in motion! If you are puzzled by this revelation, worry not, that is to be expected. All I will say to you is this, the wide-eyed among us would be advised to look a little closer. Remember what I have taught you. It's been a hoot!*

*Aunt Eliza x*

Arthur sat up and felt his heart beating in his chest. Why would his aunt leave him such a strangely worded letter in her will?

Arthur spent some time pouring over the words. 'What do you think it means, Trip?' he said to the cat who briefly looked up at him, slow-blinked his reply before he returned to grooming himself.

'Look a little closer?' Arthur muttered to himself. 'It's been a

hoot? Remember what I have taught you.' It was all very confusing, and equally puzzling too.

Eventually, he decided to do exactly what his aunt was instructing him to do. He would look a little closer. So, he grabbed his magnifying glass from his bedside table and looked all over the letter for further clues. Except he found nothing. He felt a creeping sense of despair at not being any closer to understanding what he had to do. With a heavy sigh, he folded the letter back up again. As he went to put it back in the envelope though, he saw something inside it that he hadn't seen before.

With his heart thumping excitedly in his chest, he carefully unfolded the envelope before smoothing it out flat on the bed in front of him. Scattered across the now square piece of paper, in seemingly random places, were lots of straight lines and marks. Arthur went back to the letter for further clues. Scanning the words, one line caught his eye. It was a sentence he had never heard his Aunt Eliza say before which is why it stood out, 'It's been a hoot.' The only thing he knew that hooted was an owl. But what did a bird have to do with a bit of square paper?

He picked the unfolded envelope up again and looked at the marks more closely. It was so frustrating. He knew he had the answer right there in his hands, but he was struggling to figure out what it was. As he glanced over to his bedside table, he spotted a small object.

He knew then, with complete clarity, what it was his Aunt Eliza wanted him to do. 'Of course!' he said to himself, slapping his forehead with the palm of his hand. He was annoyed with himself for not seeing it earlier.

After a couple of minutes had passed, and much folding of paper, he held in his hands the solution to his Aunt Eliza's final clue. It was something she had shown him how to make just before she'd disappeared. He didn't understand why at the time, but now it all made sense. Like the one on his bedside table, he held in his hands a paper model of an owl. When Arthur looked closer at it, he realised what all those marks were for. With the paper folded they had all come together to reveal a symbol he now recognised.

'Stay there, Trip. I'll be back soon,' he said, hastily climbing down the ladder to his bedroom and running through the carriage. Once outside, he headed towards the rusty remains of the old train engine at the other end of the yard. His parents didn't even see him as they continued to argue with one another.

As he climbed inside the rusty, old soot stained engine cab, Arthur held up the paper owl and matched the symbol on it with the one on the furnace door. He knew he was in the right place because he could see from the handle that it had been wiped clean compared with the rest of the door that was still caked in old soot.

Arthur placed the paper owl back into his pocket and with both hands he managed to pull open the heavy iron furnace door. Inside it was pitch black and as much as he tried, he couldn't see if there was anything in there or not. Nervously, Arthur put his hand in and felt around. Pushing through the many sticky cobwebs, he hoped to heavens he wouldn't put his hand on anything that moved. Just as he was considering giving up, he put his hand on a box shaped object. Without wasting another moment, he grabbed it and with all of his might he pulled it out of the furnace. As he did so, he fell backwards onto the cab's floor where he lay on his back with a bright red, soot stained suitcase on top of him.

Arthur scrambled to his feet, clutching the suitcase to his chest, and raced back to the carriage. When he got to his bedroom, he placed the suitcase down on his bed, making Trip scarper.

For a few moments, he stood and looked at the suitcase. Finally, he took a deep breath to steady his nerves, unbuckled the straps that

held it closed and flipped back the lid. Inside there were a number of items that Arthur removed and placed on his bed. Most exciting of all was another letter which he picked up. Opening it, he read:

*Dearest Arty,*

*Firstly, I must congratulate you on finding the suitcase! I knew you had it in you. Now, down to business. There are many things I wish to tell you but, because of the delicacy of what I have to say, it is best I do not divulge anything further here. Instead you will be guided to someone that will be able to help you. In the suitcase, you will find a bag of coins, a suit in your size and, most importantly of all, my old pocket watch. Keep this with you at all times.*

*At two o'clock on the afternoon of the 24th December, and if my calculations are correct that will be tomorrow, put the suit on and with the bag of coins pay for the horse and carriage that have been arranged to take you to a secret location. On arrival, you will meet*

*a very wonderful and trustworthy gentleman by the name of*
*Barnabus Cragg. He will be expecting you.*
*Best of luck!*
*Aunt Eliza x*
*P.S. Destroy this letter the first chance you get.*

Arthur put the letter down and looked at the contents of the suitcase on his bed again. He picked up his aunt's gold-plated pocket watch. It was quite a beautiful thing to behold. Engraved on the elegant casing was the same symbol that was on the front of the suitcase; an inkpot with three quills. He popped open the lid and looked inside. What he saw took his breath away. The exquisite details would have taken its highly skilled maker an incredible amount of time and effort to make. So why hadn't his aunt ever shown him it before? he thought. His Aunt Eliza loved anything mechanical and he'd never seen anything more beautiful, or well-crafted.

Inside, there was a series of golden rings that were carved and shaped to appear like layers of swirling cloud. As each one rotated, they moved slightly slower than the other, giving the appearance of the great Storm wall in motion. For a simple idea, it was incredibly effective, Arthur thought. In the middle of The Storm mechanism, gilded in gold on black stone, was a simple map of Londonian that had a crystal at its centre. Arthur was mesmerised by what he saw, and it took him some time to finally bring himself to close the lid and put everything back into the suitcase again. When the straps were tightened, he hid it under his bed so that it would be ready for the following day.

When he went to bed that night, he could hardly sleep. He could hear the gentle ticking of the pocket watch under his bed and one exciting thought stayed sharp and fresh in his mind; was he going to discover what had happened to his Aunt Eliza, and was she possibly still alive?

# CHAPTER 3

## *The Crooked Inn*

The following day, Arthur was awoken by the sound of his parents arguing in the room below him. Intrigued to know what was going on, he crept out of bed and listened in.

'Gerald Boil, you are going, and that's that,' said Mrs Boil.

'But I don't want to. I have a busy schedule,' complained Mr Boil.

'The only "schedule" you have, my dear, is to get yourself a proper job with a regular wage, just like normal people do. We need the money.'

Arthur opened the hatchway that led downstairs from his bedroom and looked down on his parents. Mrs Boil was standing in the

middle of the carriage wearing a threadbare coat, while Mr Boil was wearing a crumpled old suit with his arms crossed in defiance.

'I refuse to go!' he complained.

'Is that so? Well, I've made up my mind, and you're not going to change it… Oh, just look at your hair,' said Mrs Boil, as she tutted, licked her hands and smoothed down Mr Boil's wayward locks. Neither of them had even noticed Arthur was awake and watching them.

'Get off me, woman!' said Mr Boil, swatting Mrs Boil's hands away.

'Temper, temper!' she said, ignoring Mr Boil's childish complaints. 'See, that's much better, isn't it?'

'No, it's blooming well not. I feel like a right pudding,' he mumbled, fighting with his shirt collar as if it were strangling him. Arthur had never seen his father look so well-groomed before and he started to laugh. It was that that made both of his parents look up.

'What are you laughing at?' grumbled Mr Boil.

'Nothing,' said Arthur, trying to hold his laughter in.

'Morning, love,' said Mrs Boil, smiling up at him. 'Your father and I are going into the city to try and get him a proper job.'

'No, we're not,' complained Mr Boil.

'Yes, we are. We're probably going to be gone the whole day. Will you be all right here on your own?'

Arthur couldn't believe his luck. He didn't need to lie to his parents about where he was going today after all. 'Sure, I'll be fine,' he said.

'Hey! I could stay and look after the lad,' said Mr Boil.

'Nice try, Gerald,' replied Mrs Boil.

'Go, I'll be fine on my own,' replied Arthur. 'I'll tidy my bedroom or something.'

Mrs Boil looked up at him and raised her eyebrows. 'Really? That'll be a first.'

'There's always a first time for everything,' Arthur said, trying not to sound like he was hiding something, but knowing he was probably failing.

'Hmm,' said Mrs Boil. 'Well, you just behave yourself and don't break anything.'

'I won't,' said Arthur, returning to his room before his mother could interrogate him any further. A few minutes later he heard his parents leave.

From his bedroom window, Arthur watched his parents climb onto the old cart before the donkey pulled it out of the yard. As soon as they were out of sight, Arthur put on the suit his aunt had instructed him to wear and looked at the clock on his wall. He had less than an hour to go before the carriage arrived. He was already beginning to feel the butterflies fluttering around inside his stomach every time he thought about who he was going to meet that day. His Aunt Eliza was always full of surprises, but this was particularly strange, even by her standards.

While he waited, Arthur pulled out a box containing an assortment of bits and bobs from under his bed. Inside it was all manner of mechanical pieces, from cogs and springs to nuts and bolts, to many other weird and interesting items he had scavenged from around the train yard. His most treasured possession was a half-finished contraption he had been working on with his Aunt Eliza. Arthur removed it carefully from the box and turned it around in his hands, critiquing his handy work. It was going to be a scaled down version of his Aunt Eliza's airship when it was finished, like the one she had flown into The Storm. A sadness washed over him as it reminded Arthur of the good times they had always had together. Carefully, he put it back in the box and then slid the box under his bed. He had to hope that his Aunt Eliza would return one day to help him complete it, and he wouldn't finish it until she did.

A bell rang outside. Arthur looked out of his window and saw the horse and carriage, that had been promised, roll up in the yard. As he made his way out of the train carriage, he passed the stove and remembered what his Aunt's letter had said. From his suit jacket pocket, he retrieved the letter and threw it into the flames. Arthur watched the fire lick around the paper and the words melt away into smoke and ash. Nobody would be able to read it now, he thought. The bell outside rang again reminding him that the horse and carriage were waiting.

As soon as Arthur got inside the carriage and closed the door behind him, the well wrapped driver cracked the reins and they set off. Arthur had never ridden in such a luxurious carriage before. With its soft leather interior and fancy décor, it was a far cry from the battered old cart he was used to.

With still no idea of where he was heading to, the carriage left the yard where it began its journey along a winding dirt track. The Boils lived on the outskirts of the city, so this was as good as the streets got. It was only after a very bumpy half hour that the uneven ground flattened out as they entered into the actual city itself.

As the carriage trundled through the snowy cobbled streets of Londonian City, Arthur passed the time by looking out through the window. He was fascinated to watch the many warmly dressed Citizens walk along the brightly decorated streets, carrying in their arms their last-minute festive gifts and food. Once in a while, much to the delight of his senses, he would catch the delicious sweet smell of roasted chestnuts cooking over red-hot coals and the angelic sounds of seasonal songs sung by street corner choirs. This was a world away from the cold, grey area of Londonian he came from. It didn't matter how poor the Boils were though, they always did their best to celebrate the Winter Festival. It was the one time of the year when they could spend some time together and forget all their worries.

Arthur looked on as the bustling city passed him by. For the most part, the buildings in Londonian City were tall, crooked and imposing, and the streets below them narrow and winding. Although the streets weren't as bad as they were near his home, the cobbles made Arthur's teeth rattle in his head as the carriage weaved its way through them.

By late afternoon, the carriage passed through the great iron gates to the centre of Londonian. Arthur shuddered at the sight of the two enormous metal guards that stood either side of the gates, their faces aglow from the furnaces that roared away inside them. They stood as a reminder of The Collective's grip on Londonian and served as a warning to the Citizens about who was in charge and never to cross them.

The carriage made its way towards the main market square, a place that sat below the Victoria Point Tower. Arthur stuck his head out of the window and looked up. It hurt his neck trying to see how tall the tower actually was. The great iron structure was so gigantic that it stretched up into the clouds. He knew that somewhere up there, in her palatial office, the Prime Minister sat keeping an ever-watchful eye over the city. She rarely came down to the ground except for once a year when she would mark the opening of the Winter Festival by executing a handful of Citizens that had been found guilty of treason. A constant reminder to the Citizens that you never crossed The Collective.

It was rumoured that the Prime Minister was quite capable of stopping a person's heart just by looking at them. Not only that, most of the Citizens weren't convinced she was even human. Many had talked of seeing her fly over the city at night, like a winged demon, before returning to her nest at the top of the tower as the sun rose above The Storm (a story, no doubt influenced by her love of ravens). There were so many conflicting stories about her that nobody could ever really agree upon what the truth actually was. Arthur wasn't convinced any of them were true, but what he was sure of was that she was terrifying and should never, ever be crossed. Good people seemed to disappear that did.

Then he smelled it. Arthur coughed and placed a hand over his nose the moment he breathed in the bitter, rancid stench of the ravens. Why there were so many of these dreadful creatures in Londonian City was solely due to the Prime Minister's obsession with them. The damage they had done to the city was quite extraordinary. The acidic droppings from these worthless creatures covered nearly every conceivable surface, chewing into the stonework and making the cobbled streets dangerously greasy. Lots of the older city buildings had large lumps of the stuff hanging off them like great sticky, black icicles. Even the enormous metal guards themselves weren't immune.

As the carriage reached the great tower and was driven beneath it, Arthur found himself in what looked like the inside of a cave. Hanging from the underbelly of the tower were gigantic stalactites of petrified droppings created by the many ravens that nested in its ironwork. It was arguably the coldest, smelliest and darkest place in all of Londonian, but beneath its enormous metal legs it was home to the largest and busiest street market. For in the gloom, sat many, many stalls, lit only by the glow of the multitude of lanterns and fires that fizzed and popped away in the cold.

As the carriage weaved its way through the stalls, disembodied voices cried out in the gloom, 'Come get your onions, threepence a pound', 'Shine your shoes, only a penny,' 'Freshly baked pies, get them while they're hot.' It was almost too much for Arthur to take in. Nothing was wasted in the market either and nothing made that clearer to Arthur than when he heard a street vendor proudly shout out as they passed by, 'Get your finest raven excretions 'ere. Better than coal. Only a shilling a bag.'

The carriage continued on its journey, leaving the tower behind and making its way to the bridge that crossed over the Great River;

a body of filthy, foamy water that joined together the Eastern and Western waterfalls. On the river, there were many boats of differing sizes. Some decorated with lanterns and brightly coloured flags for the Winter Festival.

They reached the other side of the bridge and entered into the eastern side of the city. This part of Londonian was more dangerous than the western side and Arthur had never ventured this far from home before. Poking out above the rickety buildings, he saw the looming silhouette of Choke Island Prison. The place Londonian's most dangerous prisoners resided until they were cast into The Storm at the Winter Festival Riddance.

The carriage driver cracked the reins and the carriage wheels let out a squeal as it sped up. It didn't take Arthur long to realise why. They had just ventured into a frighteningly narrow alleyway in a part of the city that his parents had always warned him never to go, Nine Dials. It was where the ominous buildings loomed over the narrow cobbled streets like enormous brick giants, their structures forever threatening to fall over but never quite getting around to it. It was where the desperately poor and criminally unhinged existed, seeking refuge in a place no one else dared to go.

From amongst the shadows, the soulless faces of the unsavoury and downtrodden looked back. Arthur's eyes fixed upon a gaunt, young woman dressed in rags sitting on a cold stone step, rocking a screaming swaddled baby back and forth in her arms. She suddenly looked up at Arthur as the carriage went by. With such a haunted, pleading expression upon her face, Arthur pulled the curtain across the window, ashamed that he had ever questioned how poor he was. He was practically royalty compared to the people living in this part of the city.

For the rest of the journey, he couldn't bring himself to look out of the window again. One big question was running through his head, what sort of business did his Aunt Eliza have in such an ungodly place as this? Maybe, he thought, he didn't want to know.

The carriage took a sharp turn into another street and Arthur felt it slow down to a stop. 'Final dop,' mumbled the driver outside, before sniffing loudly.

Arthur could hear shouting. He carefully pulled back the curtain. In the growing darkness of the evening, he could make out a scrawny little man banging his fist repeatedly against a heavy wooden door. 'Open up!' the man screeched over and over again.

Arthur watched on and wondered if it would be best just to ask the driver to turn around and take him home again. Instead, and despite his better judgement, he took a deep breath, opened the door and stepped out.

'Bapple be buppence bees bir,' said the carriage driver, sniffing back a clogged-up nose as he leaned down and held out one gloved hand. Arthur fumbled around in his jacket pocket and found the bag of coins his aunt had left him, and he passed them over.

Looking up at the driver, Arthur wondered to himself how he could even move under all those layers of clothing, let alone control a horse and carriage the way he did. He counted at least six scarves, all of them wrapped around his head so tightly that Arthur could barely see his face.

'Be bareful, bir. A bangerous blace, bis is,' the carriage driver said, before he flicked the reins and headed off into the darkness leaving Arthur all alone.

'Open up, Cragg!' repeated the scrawny man.

That name he had just called out, Arthur recognised it as the name in the letter. Despite his doubts, he had found the person he was looking for after all.

'In the name of The Collective, I said open this door NOW!' demanded the scrawny man, banging on the door again.

Arthur took a deep breath and walked up behind the man before he cautiously tapped him on the shoulder. The man wasn't angry with him, so Arthur saw no reason not to speak to him. 'Excuse me, sir,' said Arthur.

The man spun around. His face was pointy, mean and furious and Arthur instantly knew who it was. 'What?' the man snapped. 'Can't you see I'm busy?'

Arthur took a step back. 'I'm sorry, Mr Spratt,' he said, 'I just wanted to know if this is where I can find Barnabus Cragg?'

'Of course, it is. He owns "The Crooked Inn". And in case you're so stupid you can't read, that's what it says up there,' said Spratt, jabbing a bony finger up at the old wooden sign above him. 'Who's asking anyway?' he asked.

'Arthur,' said Arthur.

'Arthur what?'

'Boil. Arthur Boil.'

Spratt's eyes narrowed as he appeared to be thinking. 'Son of Gerald and Lily Boil… and your now dead aunt,' he said, cackling. 'What kind of a fool flies into The Storm? Your aunt by the looks of things.'

Arthur's face flushed with anger, but he bit his lip. He wasn't going to upset this man, Spratt, any more than he already had. He'd heard plenty of stories about him, none of them good.

'What are you doing here anyway?' demanded Spratt.

'Barnabas Cragg owes me something too,' said Arthur, which wasn't exactly wrong.

'Well, he owes me first,' said Spratt 'You can have what's left if there is anything. Is that clear?'

Spratt held Arthur's stare long enough to make his threat perfectly clear. 'Did you hear me, boy?' he repeated, taking a step closer to Arthur, his fists clenched and his eyes narrowing. Arthur quickly nodded.

Just then a face appeared in one of the windows of The Crooked Inn. It was big and round and had two tufts of hair sprouting out the sides of it. It looked straight at Arthur and then disappeared again.

Spratt jabbed Arthur painfully in the chest. 'Look at me when I'm talking to you!' he growled.

The inn door flew open, hitting Spratt so hard in the face that there came a sickening snapping sound as he was sent flying backwards, knocking him out cold.

A big man filled the doorway and towered over Arthur. Arthur

stared up at him. 'Master Boil?' said the big man, and Arthur,
terrified, gulped and nodded back.

'Barnabas Cragg?' stammered Arthur.

'Yes, that's me, Master Boil, but just call me Cragg. Quick,
inside, sir!' said Cragg, looking up and down the street. 'I thoughts
you weres that horrid tax man, Horatio Spratt. Yous don't 'alf
sounds like 'im,' he said.

Before Arthur could tell Cragg that it was Spratt, he was grabbed
by his jacket lapels and pulled inside.

# CHAPTER 4
## *Barnabas Cragg*

Arthur stumbled into the inn. 'Be right with you, Master Boil,' said Cragg as he went about sliding the many iron bolts across the door, giving Arthur enough time to take in the room he now found himself in.

The first thing that struck him was how amazing it was that the place was still standing. The walls and the ceiling were at very precarious angles and as Cragg moved around, it was accompanied by some very worrying creaks and groaning sounds. All the tables and chairs were empty and, judging by the layer of dust and cobwebs on each of them, they hadn't been used in years. For an inn, it was severely lacking in customers.

In one corner, a roaring fire was popping away in the hearth but what caught Arthur's attention was the tatty looking cockerel curled up next to it. The mangy, old bird abruptly opened its one remaining eye and fixed it on Arthur. Arthur held his breath and stared back not knowing what else to do. The creature then sniffed the air, hissed at him, closed his eye again and went back to sleep.

'Well, that proves it,' said Cragg, grinning before slapping Arthur on the back, sending him stumbling forward a couple of steps.

'It has?' replied Arthur, sounding rather confused.

'Sure, it does! You've only gone and got his lordship's approval. Duke would have pecked your eyes clean out of their sockets if you'd been anyone other than Miss Eliza Monroe's nephew. You knows, he can smell your family's blood running through your veins.'

Arthur blinked then gulped. Before he could reply, there was a bang on the window and a shower of dust fell from the ceiling. A crooked-nosed face, sporting an impressively swollen eye, glared in at them.

'I'll get you for this! Just you wait,' Spratt screeched.

Cragg looked back puzzled and then at Arthur. 'What a strange looking fella. You knows 'im, Master Boil?'

'I think he's that tax collector who works for The Collective,' Arthur said.

Cragg looked surprised. 'Really? You mean Spratt?' Arthur nodded. 'Well, I didn'ts recognise him. Looks like he's had a bit of a nasty accident.'

Arthur didn't feel brave enough to tell Cragg that he was the one that had caused it.

'What does he want?' Arthur asked.

'What he always wants, Master Boil, money. The greedy so and so. Well, I ain'ts got any to give. Business hasn't exactly been good of lates.' Arthur looked around the empty inn, and at the tables and chairs covered in cobwebs.

Spratt banged on the window again. 'Open up, Cragg! You owe me money!'

'Well, I ain'ts got any, so go away or I'll set Duke on you!' Cragg shouted back. Spratt looked nervously through the window at the cockerel as it looked back at him, its eye narrowing. Before Spratt could say anything else, Cragg closed the curtains on him. 'That's better! You can see whys I always keeps the door locked, can't you?' Cragg said. 'Just to keeps that lot out.'

'He sounded angry,' Arthur said.

'He's always angry, Master Boil,' Cragg replied. 'Don't you worries yourself abouts him. Even if he gets past the locked door, he ain'ts getting past old Duke here.'

Outside Spratt roared with anger before stomping off up the street, his fists clenched at his side and one unrepeatable curse after another pouring out of his foul broken-toothed mouth.

Inside the inn, Cragg had managed to squeeze himself behind the bar. 'Before we do anything, it looks likes you could do with somethings to eat, Master Boil,' he said.

Arthur really liked the sound of that. He hadn't eaten a thing since he'd left home. 'That would be brilliant, thank you,' he said.

'Well, let's see. Maybes I could interests you in ol' Cragg's homemade soup? On the house, of course,' he said, pulling out a large pot of steaming brown gloop that had been tucked away under the bar.

Just as Arthur was about to say 'yes', the word caught in his throat as he got a whiff of it. All the colour drained from his face. Whatever that stuff was, it smelled like nothing Arthur had ever experienced before, and it wasn't pleasant. 'No! I mean, no thank you,' he managed, putting a hand over his mouth and nose. 'I've just realised, I've already eaten.'

'Really?' replied Cragg, genuinely surprised and confused, as he dipped a finger into the pot and then licked the contents off it, smacking his lips and making Arthur's stomach turn. 'Blooming marvellous. Just like me old mum used to make,' he said. 'Are you sure I can'ts tempt you?'

Arthur shook his head vigorously whilst finding it hard not to retch and he was more than grateful when Cragg finally put the pot

back under the bar.

'Well, Master Boil, we mustn't waste any more time, the evening is already upon us,' said Cragg, climbing out from behind the bar. He dropped down the hatch and another stream of dust fell from the ceiling. 'Your Aunt Eliza left me strict instructions on what to do when you arrived. Said I was to make sure I followed them to the letter,' he continued as he walked over to the fireplace and pulled on a candlestick that was sat on the mantelpiece above the fire. 'I saids to her that it would be a privilege and an honour.' Cragg choked on the last words and Arthur could see tears welling up in his eyes.

Before Arthur could ask him if he was all right, there came a series of clicking and clunking sounds and, as if by magic, the dresser moved all by itself over to one side. When it stopped, it revealed

behind it something quite unexpected. He was now looking at an old wooden door that had been hidden behind the dresser just moments earlier.

'This leads to the most important and secret of places in all of Londonian,' said Cragg, proudly.

'Really? Where does it go to?'

'You really don't know?' replied a shocked Cragg. He then smiled. 'Stupid Cragg! Of course, you wouldn't, would you?'

Arthur looked back confused.

'Don't worry Master Boil, it wouldn't be a very secret society if you did,' said Cragg.

'Secret society?' asked Arthur.

Cragg looked flustered. 'Well, er, it's not for me to say, Master

Boil.'

Arthur noted that on the door there was a carving of the same symbol that was embossed on the pocket watch his Aunt Eliza had given him. 'What does that mean?' he said, pointing at it.

Cragg relaxed and smiled back. He pulled a key on a piece of old twine from around his neck and unlocked the door with it. 'Something else you will soon learns about, Master Boil,' he said, grabbing a lit candle from the dresser before turning back to Arthur. 'We best get moving. I've already said too much.' Cragg opened the door. 'This way please, Master Boil.'

# CHAPTER 5
## *Two Important Doors*

Arthur walked towards the hidden door and stopped.

'Somethings the matter, Master Boil?' Cragg asked.

Arthur looked up and could see the genuine concern on Cragg's face and he suddenly felt guilty. His Aunt Eliza had trusted Cragg so he should too. 'There's just so much to take in,' he said.

'That's to be expected, Master Boil,' said Cragg, with a reassuring smile.

Cragg followed Arthur through the door, locking it behind them. A loud rumbling noise made Arthur jump. 'Don't you worries about that, Master Boil. That's just the dresser moving back into place,' said Cragg.

The light from the candle that Cragg was holding did little to help put Arthur at ease. He found himself standing in a tunnel where water dripped down the rough granite walls and rats scurried around in the shadows, and the dim candlelight only shone so far before the tunnel vanished into darkness again.

'If you would be so kind as to follow me, Master Boil,' said Cragg. Arthur couldn't very well back down now, so he took a deep breath and did as Cragg asked. They walked through numerous tunnels and around countless corners, Arthur hoping the whole time that the candle Cragg was holding wouldn't burn out. Finally, they turned a corner and Cragg led Arthur down a steep flight of steps. 'Nearly there,' he said. Arthur felt relieved. He was sure he'd travelled half-way across Londonian.

At the bottom, in front of them, and looking quite at odds with the dingy network of tunnels, was a lavishly decorated corridor. Although dimly lit, Arthur could make out that the stone floor had been replaced with polished wooden floorboards and the stained, cobwebbed walls were now covered with expensive handmade wallpaper and paintings.

'This way please, Master Boil,' said Cragg. As they walked past the many gilt framed paintings that seemed to occupy every free space along the walls, Arthur's curiosity got the better of him. 'Cragg, who are all these people?' he asked.

Cragg stopped and turned around, the candlelight flickering across his rosy, round face. 'Some of Londonian's most important peoples, Master Boil,' he replied, holding the candlestick up to one of the pictures so that Arthur could see it more clearly. 'This here is Dr Theodore Crampfuss.' The painting was of a dapper looking

gentleman sporting a very fine moustache that belonged to a very serious looking face. 'The distinguished Dr Crampfuss was an amazing surgeon, Master Boil. They called him Dr Lightning because, it was said, he could remove a patient's gammy leg so quickly they didn't even have time to feel the pain.'

Before Arthur could ask any more questions about him, Cragg

had turned the candle over to another painting. This time it was of an eccentric looking woman with tall, grey curly hair. In her hand, she held a splendid quill, its rainbow coloured feather belonging to a bird Arthur could not place. 'This is Madam Troutles. She studied all things paranormal, Master Boil.'

'Paranormal?' asked Arthur.

'You know Master Boil, ghosties and spirits. That sorts of thing.' Arthur felt a shiver run down his spine. As he looked down the corridor and then back at her painting, he felt sure those unblinking eyes were watching him and he quickly looked away. 'If anyone had a story to tell it was Madam Troutles, Master Boil. Her tales of haunted houses would keep you awake for many a long night.'

On the wall next to her painting, Arthur noticed there was a space where a painting had once hung. 'Whose portrait was here, Cragg?'

Cragg looked uncomfortable. 'We're not supposed to ever talks about him,' he said.

'Why?'

'He was a bad man who betrayed The Society, Master Boil.'

'Really? What was his name?'

'Well, if I tells you that, you haves to keep it to yourself?'

Arthur nodded.

'His name was Captain James Lockwood. He was once a very prominent and revered member of The Society until... well, until he dids that bad thing I said he dids, that I can'ts tell you about. Anyway, I've already said too much so let's leave it at that.'

Arthur could tell that Cragg was getting anxious talking about this man called Captain Lockwood, so he changed the subject. 'What is The Society, Cragg?' he asked.

Cragg's face dropped and he hastily turned around and started walking up the corridor again. 'We best get moving,' he said.

'Cragg?' said Arthur again, having to now half run to keep up with him.

'I'll let the others fills you in on all the details,' he said.

'What do you mean "others"?' asked Arthur, but Cragg kept on walking.

'Please, too many questions hurts me head, Master Boil. They all gets jumbled up in me brain. I is sure everything will be explained to you shortly.'

They continued to walk along the corridor until they finally reached a large, solid oak door. A door that looked robust enough to keep an army of Collective Guards at bay. 'Here we are,' said Cragg, reaching out and grabbing the big ornate brass knocker on the door. 'You wanted to know who The Society were, Master Boil? Well, you're about to find out.' He then brought the knocker down onto the door with an ear-splitting bang.

# CHAPTER 6
## *The Society*

As a clearly anxious Cragg stood before the grand oak door, it did nothing to put Arthur at ease. 'Is everything all right, Cragg?

A fidgety Cragg tried his best to give Arthur a reassuring smile. 'Oh, nothing to worry yourself about, Master Boil. I just gets a bit nervous when I is in the company of greatness, that's all. The Society are all so very clever and wise,' he said, licking his palms and attempting to smooth down his wayward hair which bounced back the moment he flattened it.

Arthur was about to ask Cragg again to explain what The Society was when a small round hole in the door opened up and an eye peered out of it.

'Cragg?' said a deep and richly upper-class voice, as the eye it was related to scanned around before it found its intended target. 'Is that you, my boy? Is everything okay?'

'Yes, sir, Mr Quilymere, sir. Master Boil has arrived, sir.'

The eye stared directly at Arthur. 'Well, bless my soul, there you are. Good heavens, my boy, haven't you grown?' said the voice.

Arthur couldn't ever remember meeting a Mr Quilymere before.

The eye glanced back at Cragg. 'Right then, I'll take it from here, thank you,' he said before turning back to Arthur. 'I'll be right with you, my boy.' The peephole shutter then snapped shut.

Cragg looked down at Arthur. 'Well, I'll be on me ways now, Master Boil,' he said.

'Are you not staying?' Arthur asked.

'It's not my place to stay, Master Boil. Sirs and Madams will look after you now,' Cragg replied. 'I just want to say that it has been a real honour meetings you, and I is so sorry to hear about what happened to Miss Eliza.' He sniffed back the tears before pulling himself together and holding out a beefy hand for Arthur to shake.

'Thank you, Cragg,' Arthur said, shaking Cragg's hand.

Cragg proudly puffed out his chest and headed off into the gloom, leaving Arthur all by himself. Standing in the cold and silent corridor waiting for Mr Quilymere to open the door, there was just enough time for Arthur to begin questioning what he was doing there. He was still struggling to imagine what sort of business his Aunt Eliza could have had in this place. He just hoped that this Mr Quilymere, whoever he was, could enlighten him.

Behind the door a series of clicking and clacking sounds echoed off the stone walls before finally they ended with a satisfying 'clonk'. For a few moments, all went quiet, before the door partly opened. Arthur was taken aback when a gentlemanly head poked out of the opening. The voice that had been big, rich and strong

was not owned by the type of person Arthur was expecting, as a short, round, balding man, fashioning an impressively thick and rather bushy moustache, smiled up at him. 'Sorry about that, my boy. Can't be too careful. The name's Tobias Quilymere. Good to see you again, Arthur,' he said, squeezing through the half-open door to shake Arthur's hand.

'Have we met before, Mr Quilymere?' asked Arthur, shaking his hand, not being able to hold the question in any longer.

Mr Quilymere chuckled. 'Oh yes, but it was many years ago when you were a very small boy. I won't hold it against you that you don't remember me. I was good friends with your wonderful aunt,' he said. He then sighed. 'It feels so wrong talking of Eliza in the past tense. I only wish we could have met under more pleasant circumstances my boy, but I'm glad you are here now.'

'Where is that exactly?' asked Arthur.

Mr Quilymere chuckled to himself again. 'Now the honest answer to that perfectly reasonable question is that none of us actually knows.'

Arthur was horrified. 'You mean you have no idea how to get back from here?' he said, glancing down into the gloom, remembering the many miles of tunnels he'd just walked through.

'No idea, whatsoever,' said Mr Quilymere. He then noticed the alarmed look upon Arthur's face. 'Oh, no need to worry, my boy. Cragg will come and get us when we're ready. He knows the way, but he's the only one. Security reasons and all that. Nobody knows this network of corridors and tunnels better than Cragg does,' he said, and then added, 'the thing is we have to be extremely careful. You see if that wretched Collective lot were to ever find out about this place. Well…' Mr Quilymere's eyes glazed over as he drifted off into his own thoughts for a moment before he shook his head and continued. 'Anyway, no point dwelling on that particularly terrifying possibility now is there?' he said.

From behind the door, a voice spoke up. 'Will you please let Master Boil in, Tobias. He must be frozen and you're letting in an awful draught!'

'Yes, yes, Eudora! I was just about to, thank you,' replied Mr Quilymere, and he rolled his eyes at Arthur. 'Well, you best come in, my boy. We have much to discuss.'

Mr Quilymere stepped to one side, so that Arthur could enter. As he passed through the doorway, Mr Quilymere quickly locked the door behind them, not that Arthur noticed as his attention had suddenly become consumed by the sight before him.

Arthur found himself standing in an elaborately decorated hexagonal shaped room. Five of the six walls were covered in row upon row of little wooden drawers, and on the remaining wall, there was a large open fireplace. On gazing up, Arthur was amazed to see a beautiful ornate chandelier that was casting the room in a wonderfully warm and magical glow. At the centre of the room, there was the familiar inkpot symbol on the floor surrounded by six comfortable looking leather armchairs; in four of them were sat some very distinguished looking ladies and gentlemen.

'Well, are you possibly going to introduce us, Tobias?' said a striking looking woman, that Arthur realised must be the person who had spoken to Mr Quilymere a moment earlier.

Mr Quilymere sighed. 'I was just about to, thank you,' he said. 'Allow me to welcome our guest. This, ladies and gentlemen, is Master Arthur Boil, nephew of Miss Eliza Monroe.'

'We know that,' snapped back the lady. 'I meant can you introduce us to Arthur. He won't know who we are.'

'Oh right, of course,' replied Mr Quilymere, before composing himself and continuing, 'This, my boy, is Madam Eudora Plummwith. Her exhaustive knowledge of herbology is unparalleled in Londonian.'

Madam Plummwith nodded in acknowledgement, a slight smile appearing on her face.

'Herby what?' said Arthur.

'Herbology,' replied Madam Plummwith. 'It means I study all things relating to plants and other associated fauna, and their uses in medicine.'

Madam Plummwith was an incredibly grand woman, both in stature and presence. Arthur would soon come to learn that everything about this mysterious, vivacious woman was larger than life. Perched atop her head, she wore an extravagant, purple tinted wig. A big enough gesture in its own right, but clearly not big enough for Madam Plummwith because she had added a gigantic peacock feather to it. While everyone else in the room wore clothes that were in muted tones and subtle in design, Madam Plummwith wore a yellow, frilly dress that was bright in contrast. She continued to regard Arthur, her eyes conveying a cool

intensity that oozed a strength and intelligence that Arthur found hypnotic, if a little intimidating. When she spoke again it was with the same wonderfully theatrical tone. 'After all these years, it is a pleasure to finally make your acquaintance, Arthur,' she said.

'Now this, my boy, is Lord Ernest Lurkybert,' said Mr Quilymere, introducing Arthur to quite an eccentric looking gentleman. He had a ruddy complexion and wore a cream coloured suit, reserved it always seemed for gentlemen who did a lot of travelling. Before

Arthur could speak, Lord Lurkybert had shot to his feet and saluted. 'General Ernest Lurkybert reporting for duty, sir!' he said.

Arthur didn't know what to say. He peered over at the other Society members for help, but they appeared quite embarrassed by Lord Lurkybert's antics. Only Madam Plummwith sat with her lips pursed in annoyance. Without being able to think of anything else to do, Arthur saluted back. This seemed to work. Lord Lurkybert acknowledged the gesture with a brief smile and removed his hand from his forehead before shaking Arthur's hand with it. 'Pleased to meet you, laddie,' he said.

'Lord Lurkybert has travelled to the furthest reaches of Londonian, many times over, and has seen plenty of wonderful and mysterious things,' continued Mr Quilymere.

'No way! Really?' said Arthur, not being able to contain his excitement.

Lord Lurkybert's moustache twitched, a proud smile appearing beneath it. 'Mr Quilymere is quite right, laddie. I've explored the Wailing Woods and stood at the base of both the Eastern and Western Waterfalls. Ruddy great racket they make I can tell you. I got quite wet too,' he said.

'So, amazing!' replied Arthur, really meaning it. 'You've actually travelled everywhere in Londonian then?'

'That I have. I'd be travelling further afield if it wasn't for that blooming Storm,' he replied.

Arthur thought that was a very strange thing to say. It was common knowledge that there was nothing beyond The Storm, everyone knew that. It wasn't called The Nowhere for nothing.

'Anyway, laddie, it's a pleasure to meet you,' Lord Lurkybert continued. 'I see your aunt's features in yours. You have that same white streak in your hair just like she did, what?'

Mr Quilymere turned to another one of The Society members. 'This fellow is the distinguished Mr William Hardgrave,' he said. Mr Hardgrave was a rather extravagant looking gentleman. There was a lot of velvet and silk to his suit which perfectly complemented the twirly beard and moustache that graced his dour looking face. Arthur held out his hand for Mr Hardgrave to shake, but instead of shaking it, he gave his own wrist a theatrical flick. A puff of purple smoke flashed before Arthur's eyes and, as it dissipated, Mr Hardgrave held in his hand a golden playing card, seeming to have magically appeared out of nowhere.

Arthur gingerly took the card. Written upon it, in flamboyant,

curvaceous handwriting, was a name. Arthur read it out aloud. 'The Great Martini?' he said.

Mr Hardgrave nodded graciously. 'That is I,' he replied. 'The second greatest magician in all of Londonian.'

'The second greatest?' asked Arthur.

'I must concede that honour goes to the mysterious person who conjured up The Storm,' replied Mr Hardgrave.

'Why are you always so quick to assume it is some sort of stupid man-made magic trick?' said Madam Plummwith. 'If there's one thing I have learnt over the years studying the natural world, it is this, always expect the unexpected.'

'You must excuse, Eudora. It's all rather quaint, but she believes that The Storm was created by some mystical force,' Mr Hardgrave said, smirking.

'I said no such thing,' snapped back Madam Plummwith. 'I only stated that there are still a great many things to learn about our world. So, you stick to your silly magic trick theory and I'll keep an open mind.'

Mr Quilymere stepped in before things escalated. 'Master Boil, you must understand that Mr Hardgrave and Madam Plummwith have, shall we say, very differing views on how The Storm came to be,' he said.

'So I see,' Arthur replied.

'I have made it my life's work to discover how the illusion of The Storm is accomplished,' said Mr Hardgrave.

'That may be William, but Eudora believes there is something more at play,' said Mr Quilymere.

'It is not a matter of belief but a matter of one keeping a very open mind about how little we really know about this world,' replied Madam Plummwith, shooting Mr Hardgrave a challenging look before continuing. 'Some like to naively believe that we have educated ourselves on all that is left to be learnt. There are a great many mysterious things in this world that are yet to be discovered, Arthur. I can't tell you what they are, but there lies the excitement of discovery. You must remember that we have always challenged our beliefs throughout history and, without fail, we have constantly surprised ourselves and expanded our knowledge in the process. It is only when we accept our limitations that we can go beyond them.'

'Thank you, William and Eudora,' Mr Quilymere cut in before Mr Hardgrave could reply. 'Master Boil has yet to meet our last member. So, if you don't mind?' Mr Hardgrave and Madam

Plummwith shot each other disapproving looks but did indeed go quiet. Mr Quilymere cleared his throat and turned to the most curious member sat before Arthur. 'And finally, this is Miss Ida Quilymere,' said Mr Quilymere, smiling. 'She's my niece.'

Ida stopped sketching in her notebook and turned around in her chair. It was the first chance Arthur had got to see her properly and

he was taken aback. Her pure white hair contrasted starkly with her youthful appearance and it was for this reason, Arthur realised, why he hadn't noticed how young she was when he had walked into the room. When their eyes met, Arthur couldn't look away. The pupils of Ida's large almond shaped eyes were bright ruby red and her skin was chalk white. Arthur tried to speak but the words just got stuck in his throat.

Ida turned to Mr Quilymere. 'Is he all right?' she asked, genuinely concerned.

'I don't know,' Mr Quilymere said. 'Arthur?'

Arthur snapped out of his trance. 'Sorry, I...' he tried, but he stumbled on his words, 'I mean, there's been a lot to take in.'

'Of course, my boy,' said Mr Quilymere.

'Well, it's nice to meet you, Arthur,' Ida said, smiling politely up at him.

'Ida lives with me. Tragically, she lost her parents at an early age. Terrible fire. Quite, quite awful,' Mr Quilymere said.

Arthur didn't know how to respond so he ended up saying the only thing he thought would be acceptable. 'I'm sorry,' he said.

'That's okay,' said Ida. 'I can't remember anything about what happened to my parents. Thankfully, I can't recall anything from that far back in my life anyway which I guess is probably for the best.'

Mr Quilymere took Ida's hand and smiled at her. 'Quite right my dear. Something that ghastly is best left in the past,' he said. He then turned back to Arthur. 'Well, there you have it my boy, that's all of us,' he said. 'Please, do take a seat. We have much to discuss and the evening is drawing on.'

# CHAPTER 7
## *The Dedication Table*

'Over there, Arthur, was where your Aunt Eliza used to sit,' Mr Quilymere said, pointing to an empty, green leather chair by the fire. 'Every year, on this very day, she would spend the evening sitting in that chair, feverishly taking notes.' Mr Quilymere sighed. 'Such a tragic loss. She was a wonderful woman with a head full of so many amazing and exciting ideas.'

Arthur managed a smile. That sounded exactly like his Aunt Eliza, he thought. Arthur's mother used to tell him that Eliza was so dedicated to her engineering interests that she felt sure she had oil running through her veins instead of blood.

Mr Quilymere put a hand on Arthur's shoulder. 'I can't begin to imagine how sad you must be feeling, my boy,' he said. 'It has come as a great shock to us all. She was a most cherished member of The Society, Arthur,' he said. 'We shall all miss her dearly.'

'Hear! Hear!' said Lord Lurkybert.

'Was she important in your society?' asked Arthur.

'Oh, my goodness, absolutely,' replied Madam Plummwith. 'She was what we call the Grand Scribe. The most prestigious position held by any member.'

'I had no idea until today that she was even in a society, let alone being a Grand Scribe, whatever that is,' said Arthur.

'And so you shouldn't have,' said Mr Hardgrave. 'No member of this society ever talks about it outside these walls. It is strictly forbidden. What we have to say within this room, stays within this room. Always. That code of silence now extends to yourself, boy. So, don't go blabbing about this place to anyone else or you'll get us all killed.'

Before Arthur could reply, Madam Plummwith spoke up, 'You

really can't help being rude, can you William?'

'I am merely informing the child of the dangers,' said Mr Hardgrave.

'Child?' snapped back Madam Plummwith. 'His name is Arthur or Master Boil.'

'I'll call him what I like, thank you,' replied Mr Hardgrave.

'In that case, I'll start calling you by the name that I think best suits you, and you certainly won't like that.'

Before the argument could spiral out of control, Mr Quilymere cut in. 'All right everyone! Let's move on, shall we?' he said. Mr Hardgrave and Madam Plummwith shot each other hate-filled stares, but they did at least do as Mr Quilymere had requested.

'May I suggest,' continued Mr Quilymere, 'Arthur takes his place in his aunt's old chair. It does feel right that he should now be its rightful owner,' he said.

'Hear, hear!' Lord Lurkybert said again, this time raising the glass in front of him to show his approval.

'I'm sure it's what your aunt would have wanted, Arthur,' said Ida smiling at him.

Arthur sat down. He was struck by an overwhelming sense of familiarity as he got a whiff of the subtle but familiar aromas of old engine grease, coal and wet paint. It was as if his Aunt Eliza was in the room with him. He felt his eyes begin to cloud up as tears threatened to bubble to the surface and it took him an awful lot of willpower to stop them from falling.

'Comfortable?' Mr Quilymere asked Arthur as he sat down in the remaining empty chair the other side of the fireplace.

'Perfect,' replied Arthur, and he meant it.

Mr Quilymere poured himself a glass of ginger ale and one for Arthur too. 'I hope you don't think this discourteous, my boy, but would you mind if we ask you a few questions?' he said.

'That's fine,' said Arthur, taking a sip of his ginger ale.

Madam Plummwith cut in before Mr Quilymere got a chance to speak. 'If I may, Tobias?' she said.

'Be my guest, Eudora,' he replied.

'We were all hoping that you may be able to shed some light on what happened to your poor aunt, Arthur,' she said. 'It seemed quite out of character for her to have done something quite so, well, now how can I put this…'

'Reckless?' Mr Hardgrave said.

'Do you mind!' Madam Plummwith snapped back.

'That's what you were thinking.'

'It most certainly was not.'

'Aunt Eliza wasn't like that,' Arthur said, jumping to his aunt's defence. 'She was one of the cleverest, bravest people I know.'

'That is what makes this whole tragic affair all the more curious,' said Mr Quilymere.

'It goes without saying, Arthur, that we all agree with you. Even Mr Hardgrave. Isn't that right William?' said Madam Plummwith, shooting Mr Hardgrave an angry look and daring him to disagree.

'Well, laddie, for what it's worth, I think what she did was blooming heroic,' said Lord Lurkybert.

'I agree, but I only wish she had told us what she was intending to do. We would have had a chance to convince her it was foolhardy and dangerous,' said Mr Quilymere.

'Then that is quite possibly why she didn't tell us,' said Madam Plummwith.

As she looked over at Arthur, it was obvious to him that Madam Plummwith, and the other Society members, were all hoping he had some more information to give. 'I'm sorry,' he said, 'but, Aunt Eliza didn't tell me anything either.'

Mr Quilymere sighed. 'That's quite all right, my boy,' he said, but Arthur could tell from his expression he was disappointed.

'Oh, come on, you must take us for fools, boy,' said Mr

Hardgrave, the venom in his voice catching Arthur off guard. 'Are you really expecting us all to believe that you never asked your aunt why she was building a hot air balloon?' he said. 'I should have imagined that would have been a rather obvious question to ask, wouldn't you agree?'

'I knew she was building a balloon. I just didn't know what for,' replied Arthur, his face feeling hot. 'I never thought she'd fly it into The Storm like that. I would have stopped her myself if I did. I'm not lying to you, I promise.'

'Don't worry, my boy, we believe you,' said Mr Quilymere.

Ida looked up from her notebook. 'Can you remember anything else she might have said to you though, Arthur?'

'Whenever I asked, she just said, "you'll see", and then changed the subject,' Arthur replied.

'And you didn't push her for more answers?' said Mr Hardgrave.

'No, because I'm not rude,' said Arthur.

Madam Plummwith chuckled at that comment as Mr Hardgrave's eyes narrowed. 'Well, it's quite clear to me she was protecting you,

Arthur,' Madam Plummwith said.

'Protecting me? From what?'

The room went quiet as guarded looks were exchanged between The Society members. Mr Quilymere eventually spoke up. 'You must try and understand that your aunt didn't tell you what she was doing because she couldn't. There was nothing you could have done to have changed her mind. It is clear that she wanted to do what she did on her own. So, don't you believe for a moment that any of this is your fault,' he said, shooting Mr Hardgrave a look that dared him to disagree.

'What was my aunt protecting me from?' Arthur replied.

'As I'm sure you are aware, it is quite possible for a person to know too much in Londonian,' said Madam Plummwith. 'It is the very reason we, The Society, hide ourselves down here.'

'But what exactly is The Society?' Arthur asked.

'All in good time, Arthur,' said Mr Quilymere, 'because we must begin tonight's meeting. The evening is rolling on.' Before Arthur had a chance to ask any more questions, Mr Quilymere continued, 'I believe you have on your possession your aunt's Emblem. Can I have it, please?'

Arthur looked very worried. 'I don't have anything like that,' he said.

Mr Quilymere's brow furrowed. 'Oh, I see. That complicates things somewhat,' he said.

Madam Plummwith smiled. 'Eliza's pocket watch, Tobias,' she said.

Mr Quilymere's face brightened, and he relaxed. 'Of course, thank you Eudora. Do you have that on you, Arthur?'

Arthur did. He went to his jacket pocket and retrieved it, before handing it over to Mr Quilymere.

'Now let's see if I remember how this goes,' he said, flipping open the case. Looking through his monocle, he began twisting The

Storm decorations, one way then the other, until there came a delicate click and it opened up. 'Hah! There we go,' he said, smiling. Mr Quilymere passed the watch over to Arthur. Inside Arthur could now see his aunt's Emblem. 'You can't keep something this valuable safe enough, my boy,' he said. 'To say that this room has some of the most precious and dangerous artefacts in all of Londonian is an understatement.'

'Mr Quilymere is right,' said Madam Plummwith. 'Between these walls are many, many items that must never be spoken of in this city,' she said. 'If The Collective were to ever find this place, they would destroy everything in it, including us.'

'But what can be as dangerous as all that?' Arthur asked, just before he took a large swig of his drink.

'Proof that beyond The Storm wall there lies another world,' said Ida, not even looking up from her notebook.

Arthur was so shocked at what Ida had just said that he spat out his mouthful of ginger ale, showering Mr Hardgrave, who was sat opposite him, with it. Nobody moved, not even Mr Hardgrave. He sat there, staring viciously at Arthur, ginger ale running down his face. Arthur watched on terrified waiting to see what Mr Hardgrave would do next. Instead of shouting like Arthur expected, he silently pulled out a string of multicoloured handkerchiefs from one sleeve and slowly wiped his face clean. Arthur could see out of the corner of his eye that Madam Plummwith was smirking.

'Sorry,' said Arthur, but before Mr Hardgrave could reply Arthur quickly turned to the other Society members, 'A world beyond The Storm? Are you sure?'

'Absolutely, my boy,' Mr Quilymere replied. 'We collect stories and artefacts from the Old World and keep them safely here. Or, to put it another way, objects that existed from a time before The Storm.'

'But that's impossible!' said Arthur.

'I can assure you that it isn't?' said Mr Quilymere.

A thought then crossed Arthur's mind. 'You think that's where Aunt Eliza has gone, don't you?'

'We didn't say that,' said Mr Quilymere before he took a deep breath and continued, 'the truth is, we just don't know, but, yes, it is a possibility.'

'Then there's a chance she could still be alive?' said Arthur.

'Don't be so hasty, Arthur,' said Madam Plummwith. 'Nobody has ever flown into The Storm before and survived.'

'But my aunt isn't just anybody, is she?' said Arthur. 'She's Eliza Monroe.'

'Quite right, laddie!' said Lord Lurkybert. 'If anyone can beat that ruddy great Storm, well I'd put my last farthing on your aunt doing it.'

'Wherever she is, there is nothing we can do for her now,' said Mr Quilymere. 'All we can do is hope that she will possibly return to us one day.'

'One thing we can certainly promise you Arthur, if she does return, we will be here for her,' said Madam Plummwith.

'While we wait for just such a day, I'm sure you would like to know a little more about The Society? Now that you are a member that is,' said Mr Quilymere.

'A member?' Arthur said.

'It was your aunt's wishes that you take her place in such an event that she could not continue with her involvement in The Society.' said Mr Quilymere.

Arthur didn't know what to say.

'Is that okay with you, Arthur?' asked Madam Plummwith. 'Eliza said that she couldn't think of anyone more worthy.'

Arthur felt everyone's eyes looking at him while they waited to hear what he had to say next. He was a Boil by name, but his veins ran with Monroe blood, and Monroes never turned around in the face of adversity. 'Yes, it will be an honour,' he said.

'Good show!' said Lord Lurkybert.

'Welcome aboard, my boy,' said Mr Quilymere. 'Now you're a fully-fledged member, is there anything you'd like to know?'

Arthur looked around the room and his eyes rested on all the tiny drawers. 'Can you tell me more about those?' he asked.

Madam Plummwith smiled. 'Ah! The Artefactary, of course. They hold the rarest and most prized collection of items in the whole of Londonian,' she said. 'Each one of those drawers holds an item or historical document relating to The Other Lands beyond The Storm. Everything The Society members have brought along with them over the years is in one of those drawers.'

'But there must be hundreds of them,' Arthur said, craning his neck to look around him.

'Actually, they number in their thousands, Arthur,' said Mr Quilymere, proudly. 'Three thousand, two hundred and seventy-five to be precise. In the beginning, every Winter Festival Eve, this room would be full of people like us, ready to add to the collection you see around you. Sadly though, today that number has diminished, and we and the items in those drawers are all that is left of The Society. Holding onto the truth has become much more difficult as time has gone by.' Arthur watched on while Mr Quilymere became lost in his own thoughts as he looked deep into the open fire.

'The question is, are you willing to side with the truth or be a naive fool and just accept the lies?' said Mr Hardgrave.

'Enough William, there's no need to be so dramatic,' said Mr Quilymere. 'Even if, on this occasion, you are possibly right.' There was a moment's silence before Mr Quilymere spoke again, 'Well, unless anyone has any objections, we should get things under way.'

Before Arthur could ask what he meant, Mr Quilymere pulled up one of the armrests on his chair. To Arthur's surprise, it revealed a small, round, brass button underneath it. Mr Quilymere looked at Arthur. 'I think you're going to like this bit,' he said, pushing the button. The whole floor started to rumble. In the middle of the room, the symbol on the floor dropped down and slid to one side leaving an opening. Through it, a decorative wooden hexagonal shaped table with brass ornate trimmings and a golden quill at its centre rose up. When it stopped moving, Mr Quilymere flipped down his chair's armrest and turned and smiled at Arthur. 'I bet you didn't expect that, did you?' he said.

Arthur looked at Mr Quilymere, his mouth wide open. He had never seen anything quite like it before. Although he couldn't see its workings, Arthur knew that under the table there had to be an intricate arrangement of cogs and pulleys to drive a contraption as elaborate as this.

'This, my boy, is the Dedication Table,' said Mr Quilymere. 'It will indicate which one of us will be nominated to tell a story about The Other Lands.'

Arthur looked down at the table and noted that from its centre there were six brass gullies that snaked to the table's outer edge. At the end of each of the gullies was a circular indentation. Mr

Quilymere went to his waistcoat pocket, retrieved his Emblem and placed it into the indentation nearest to him. All of the other Society members followed suit. 'To activate the Table, all of the Emblems must be in place, Arthur,' said Mr Quilymere.

Arthur felt a swell of pride as he took the Emblem out of his aunt's pocket watch and placed it in the indentation on the table in front of him. No sooner had he done so, there was a hissing sound and the clinking and clacking of invisible cogs and gears. This time the golden quill in the middle of the table started to rotate on its nib. The Society members all sat forward and eagerly watched it. Moments later it stopped and tipped over. A bright green liquid ran down one of the gullies until it encircled one of the Emblems.

'Ah! Well, it does appear that you shall be starting things off this evening, Mr Hardgrave,' said Mr Quilymere, then added, 'I do hope we can expect a story of a less bleak nature than usual this time, William.'

Mr Hardgrave gave a wry smile and without replying he closed his eyes. He then took a deep breath, reopened his eyes and began, 'Ladies and gentlemen, I shall now tell you all a story about an interesting prince and his unquenchable thirst for blood.'

'Not again,' Mr Quilymere mumbled.

# CHAPTER 8
## *Flob*

As Mr Hardgrave began to recount his gruesome story, a very livid Spratt was stomping through the cold busy streets of Londonian muttering to himself. As soon as anyone saw him coming, they jumped out of his way or crossed the street. Everyone

in Londonian knew he was a nasty, sadistic, little creature who wouldn't think twice about dishing out some loathsome punishment just for the fun of it, especially when he was in the mood he was currently in.

A small boy, still too young to know who Spratt was, bounced a ball in the street while his mother looked in through a shop window. Lost in his own little world, the boy didn't see Spratt as he came bounding around the corner. But Spratt had seen him, and he was in no mood to stop. 'Get out of my way, you snivelling brat!' he screeched. Before the small boy knew what was happening, Spratt had shoved him to one side knocking him painfully to the hard, cobbled stones.

The moment the boy's mother heard her son scream, she spun around. 'The nasty man pushed me over,' squealed the boy, pointing at Spratt.

If he hadn't had his back to her, and if only she had recognised who she was about to shout at, she would never have done what she did next. 'Oi! You! What do you thinks you're playing at?' she yelled. As she tried to comfort her now sobbing son, Spratt stopped dead in his tracks and slowly turned around. It was only then, when she looked into his crazed feral eyes, did she realise what she had just done. 'Oh no,' she said to herself, a cold chill of dread shooting down her spine.

'You have something you want to say to me, Citizen?' he said, hanging onto that last word as if it revolted him to say it. Those Citizens that were between Spratt and the woman hastily got out of the way. With his fists clenched, he began walking slowly towards her.

The woman cowered, and she quickly put her son protectively behind her. 'It was a mistake. I'm sorry. It won't happen again,' she said.

'Oh, you can bet your pitiful life, it won't.'

The woman held her breath as Spratt stopped just in front of her. 'You dare to speak to me like that...' he said, his eyes narrowing over his crooked nose while he appeared to think, 'Veronica Sliplace.'

Veronica looked up horrified.

'You think I don't know who you are?' said Spratt. 'I know the name of every one of your pitiful kind in this city. Especially sewer scum like you.'

Although she was angry, she couldn't help the tears that were now rolling down her cheeks.

Spratt held out a hand. 'Give me that bag,' he said.

Veronica looked down at the shopping in her hands, full of the next day's festive food. She turned back to Spratt, a pleading look on her face. 'Please, Mr Spratt,' she said, 'it's the eve of the Winter Festival. It has taken me all year to save for this one meal.'

'Hand it over!' he demanded, snatching the bag from her hand. Before Veronica knew what was happening, Spratt had turned the bag upside down and emptied the contents onto the floor. 'Oops,' he said with a smirk on his face. 'I'm such a butterfingers. You best pick that up before I have you arrested for littering.' As Veronica went to bend down to do as she was told, Spratt started jumping up

and down on the food until all that was left on the filthy floor was an inedible mulch. When he was satisfied that he had destroyed everything, he stopped and looked straight into Veronica's alarmed eyes, a gruesome smirk on his face. 'Well, pick it up then,' he said, throwing the now empty bag back at her.

Spratt turned around and carried on up the street, leaving Veronica to scoop up the remains of her family's festive meal. That had put him in a slightly better mood, there was no doubt about that. What he had just done to Veronica Sliplace though was nothing compared to what he had planned for Mr Barnabus Cragg. For that punishment, he would need to call on the services of his only trusted colleague, Flob.

When Spratt eventually reached the building he was looking for, a giant hand stopped him at the door. A bulking hulk of a man, whose enormous frame was squeezed into an ill-fitting suit, looked down at him. 'Identity,' he said, in a deep, gravelly voice.

Spratt looked up and growled before kicking the doorman in the shins. He howled out in pain. 'It's me you imbecile,' said Spratt.

As the doorman hopped around on one leg, he suddenly clocked who he was dealing with and swiftly hopped to one side while bowing and saluting at the same time. 'I is sorry sir. I didn't recognise you, Mr Spratt, sir,' he said.

Spratt grunted disapprovingly, shoved past him and went inside. The place was packed with people and a thick choking smog from the fire filled the claustrophobic inn. Well-to-do ladies and gentlemen were relaxing while a jaunty Winter Festival song was being played on the upright piano by an old ruddy faced gentleman. The place was very raucous but very much brimming with festive cheer and Spratt despised it. As he pushed his way through the crowded room, those that were unlucky enough to catch a look at him recoiled in horror and disgust. 'Flob!' Spratt called out, but it was clear he wasn't going to be heard over the noise. So, he filled his lungs and tried again. 'QUIET!' he shrieked.

The room fell deathly silent. Even the pianist was left with his fingers hovering over the keys, not daring to play another note. From the back of the room, a deep and stupid voice broke the silence. 'Spratt?' said Flob, holding a half empty tankard of root beer in his hand, a foamy white moustache sitting below his bulbous crooked nose.

The crowd hastily parted as Spratt made his way over to him. 'Where were you?' he screeched. 'While I was out there working, you were in here… getting merry.'

Flob, sitting at a ridiculously small table for his gigantic size, looked rather terrified. 'No, it's not what it looks like, I swears,' said Flob, forgetting he was still holding the tankard in his hand.

'It's exactly what it looks like,' Spratt spat back.

The other customers were now turning to one another and

whispering. Without any warning Spratt spun around to face them. 'You lot got anything to say?' he said.

They all quickly looked away and tried their best to get back to what they were doing. There wasn't one person in that inn that didn't know who Spratt was. He may have been physically small and weedy but his notorious reputation and influence within The Collective was infamous. The man at the piano started to play again and the room returned to the noisy atmosphere of moments earlier.

'What happened to your face?' asked Flob. 'Your nose is all wonky.' Without thinking Flob leant over the table and grabbed Spratt's crooked nose and, with a toe-curling crack, snapped it back into position.

For a second, Spratt's eyes watered before he finally let out a blood-curdling scream. All eyes glanced around but quickly looked away again when they saw how furious Spratt was. He turned to Flob who flinched. 'What do you think you are doing?' he yelped.

'It needed fixing, so I fixed it,' Flob said, cowering. 'I thought you'd be happy.'

Spratt leant over and snatched the tankard out of Flob's hand before downing what remained of the lukewarm liquid and slamming the empty tankard down on the table in front of him. 'You said you want to know what happened?' said Spratt, and Flob nodded. 'Well, while you were in here having a merry old time, a jumped-up Citizen scum thought he would assault me, that's what.'

Flob's face darkened. 'Who was it?' he said.

'That scruffy old inn keeper, Barnabas Cragg,' said Spratt.

Flob's slab-like brow lifted up in surprise. 'He runs that Crooked Inn place, don't he?' he said. 'He ain't got it in 'im, surely?'

Spratt's eye twitched and pointed at his broken face. 'Does this look like he doesn't?' he said.

Flob stood up, towering way above Spratt. He then grabbed the empty tankard from the table and crushed it in his hands as if it was made of nothing more than paper. 'I say we pays him a visit,' he said.

For the first time since he'd walked into the inn, a wicked smile spread across Spratt's nasty little face. 'Now you're talking my language,' he said.

# CHAPTER 9

## *So Many Stories*

Mr Hardgrave finished his story, crossed his arms and sat back in his chair.

'Right,' Mr Quilymere said, breaking the silence that followed. 'That was, erm, vivid, William.'

While the other Society members looked mildly disturbed by Mr Hardgrave's tale, Arthur had sat transfixed. He found himself completely lost in the world that Mr Hardgrave had painted with its castles and bizarre cast of characters. Now that it was over, he desperately wanted to know more, but before he could ask him any questions, Lord Lurkybert spoke up. 'Romania eh, old boy? A place I would very much like to travel to one day,' he said.

'It is also somewhere I intend to visit myself as soon as we can leave this wretched city,' replied Mr Hardgrave.

The room went quiet and Arthur finally got his chance to speak. 'Where did you get that story from?' he said.

'We have our ways,' replied Mr Hardgrave. 'Even though those dreadful Collective fools have tried to remove all memory of The Other Lands, there are still fragments left to be discovered. That is, if you know where to look.'

Despite the fact they were in a hidden room, miles below Londonian, just hearing someone openly criticise The Collective made Arthur uneasy. 'Why have they hidden the truth from everyone for all these years?' Arthur asked.

Mr Quilymere looked at him. 'Now there is a story,' he said.

'Will you tell it to me?'

'It would be my pleasure, my boy,' said Mr Quilymere, taking a sip of his drink. 'Two hundred years ago, when The Storm first appeared, most of the inhabitants of Londonian were terrified at being trapped inside the eye of a storm. But there were also those that saw it as an opportunity. A group made up of criminal bosses and corrupt politicians worked together to gain control of the city and create the dreaded party we know today as The Collective. To do this, they had to remove the one thing that they knew would make the people fight back.'

'What was that?' Arthur asked.

'Knowledge,' said Mr Quilymere. They planned on erasing all memory of The Other Lands forever.'

'But, why?'

'The Collective knew they had the city under their power, but they didn't know for how long,' said Ida, continuing to draw in her notebook. If they didn't make the Citizens forget about The Other Lands, then The Collective believed they would soon tire of Londonian and try to find a way to leave it.'

'So, how did they change so many people's minds?' asked Arthur.

'What they did next was so horrifying that it was supposed to have been erased from history. But the truth always has a way of surviving. They gathered everything they could find that was related to The Other Lands; all manner of objects including pictures, maps, books, even plants. It wasn't long before the pile of artefacts was as tall as a hundred houses, maybe more. As the Citizens stood around, surrounded by an army of Collective Guards, they watched on in horror, helpless as The Collective set it alight. It burned for ten days and ten nights until all that was left was a giant mound of ash,' Mr Quilymere said, leaning over and prodding the fire with a poker. Arthur watched as the fire released hundreds of little embers that twisted and twirled up the chimney. It made him think of how terrible it must have been to have witnessed something so destructive; all that knowledge, history and art gone up in flames forever.

'They destroyed everything that reminded people there was a

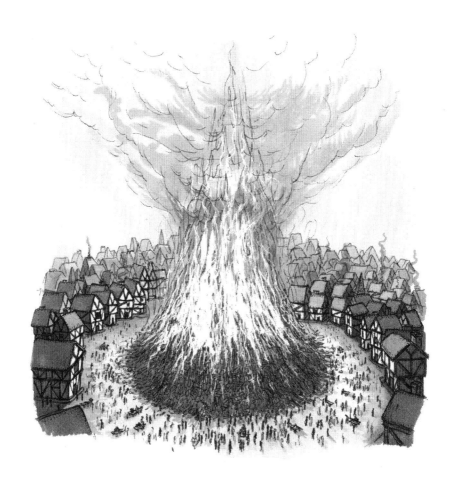

world beyond The Storm,' Ida added, 'and then made it a crime to ever speak of The Other Lands again.'

'We call that moment in history "The Day of Ignorance",' Madam Plummwith said.

'It amazes me how easy it is to convince people of something so blatantly wrong. Persuasion, it seems, is a more potent force than truth,' said Lord Lurkybert.

Madam Plummwith muttered in agreement.

'And do you know what the worst thing to happen was?' Mr Quilymere asked Arthur, and he shook his head in response.

'It actually worked,' Mr Hardgrave replied.

'Sadly, Mr Hardgrave is correct,' said Madam Plummwith. 'Almost everyone soon forgot what the real name of "The Other Lands" was, knowing it from then on only as…'

'The Nowhere,' interrupted Arthur.

'Exactly,' said Mr Quilymere.

'So, none of it's true?'

'What worth does the truth have if you are willing to accept the lies?' said Madam Plummwith.

'But they didn't destroy everything though, did they?' said Arthur. 'This room is full of stories and artefacts from The Other Lands.'

'That is something to be thankful for,' Mr Quilymere said, 'but this is almost all that is left.'

'Then we must let all of the Citizens of Londonian know. We can fight back against The Collective,' said Arthur, sitting forward in his chair.

The Society members went quiet.

'Come on! We must do something?' he said.

'If only it were that easy, Arthur,' said Mr Quilymere.

'But it is!' said Arthur.

'Ah, my boy. You are so much like you Aunt Eliza. She never stopped fighting either.'

'And we shouldn't too,' Arthur replied.

'Sadly, it is far too dangerous now,' replied Mr Quilymere. 'The Prime Minister has a grip on this city like never before and our numbers are too few. She has her army of Guards and all we have is each other.'

Madam Plummwith turned to Arthur, 'Those that have tried in the past have risked the very existence of The Society and were killed in the process. It's the very reason the Prime Minister knows that The Society exists, but thankfully she has never discovered our whereabouts.'

Arthur's mind and heart raced. Ida leant over and put her hand on his and he felt a rush of calm flow through his whole body. 'We all feel the same as you, Arthur. One day we will reveal the truth, but now is not the time,' she said. 'All we can do is hope and, through us, keep the memory of The Other Lands alive. For as long as we know of their existence, the Prime Minister hasn't won.'

Arthur nodded, but he still felt troubled. He sat back in his chair, his head now whirling like The Storm itself.

'Right then, shall we continue?' said Mr Quilymere, lifting up his chair's armrest and pushing the button underneath it again.

Arthur watched the golden quill spin on its pivot and he now knew that he had to learn more about the world beyond The Storm. In Arthur's mind, he had begun to take on the most challenging puzzle he had ever been presented with. He needed to find a way to rid Londonian of The Collective and then destroy The Storm.

# CHAPTER 10
## *Cragg Gets A Visit*

Cragg spat onto the counter of the bar and then, with his trusty old rag, he wiped it down until it shone. 'Well, it's almost Winter Festival Day, me ol' feathered friend,' he said. Duke lazily opened his one good eye. He then ruffled his shaggy feathers before shutting it again. He didn't reply but that didn't matter to Cragg. He knew that Duke was more of a listener than a talker. Cragg placed his old rag back on the counter and sat down on a stool.

With the inn cleaned and nothing else to do, Cragg went to his trouser pocket and pulled out an old crumpled-up piece of paper. As he unfolded it, a woman with a mop of curly black hair smiled back. Tears welled up in Cragg's eyes as he looked down at the portrait of Eliza Monroe. 'I misses her so much,' he said to Duke. He didn't even open his eye this time, but that was fine, Cragg knew he was still listening. 'Oh Eliza, I nevers even got to tell you how much I loves you,' he said, running a plump thumb gently over Eliza's cheek. Cragg had never said anything to Eliza in all the years he had known her. He had never been brave enough to. The moment she had first walked into his little inn, he had fallen head over heels in love with her. Cragg whimpered, tears running down his face. He picked up the old rag from the counter and blew his nose on it. He then folded the piece of paper back up and put it carefully back inside his trouser pocket.

Cragg looked over at the dresser and started to wonder how this year's Society meeting was going. He remembered sitting where he was now as a small boy while his father went about his duty as The Society Guardian, an honour that had now been bestowed upon himself. His father had seen many different Society members over the years turn up every Winter Festival Eve ready to be guided down the tunnels. His father had told him that there was indeed a time when there had been members of The Society that could recount stories they'd actually witnessed first-hand themselves.

Although the mere mention of The Other Lands was forbidden in Londonian, The Society members knew that The Crooked Inn was also a place they could talk openly about such things. The discussions were supposed to go on behind closed doors but when some had had a few drinks it loosened their tongues and they would talk a little too openly in front of Cragg. As a child, he was constantly enthralled by what he heard; tales of animals as big as houses with long bendy noses and gigantic ears; of creatures with necks that stretched to the very clouds themselves, if you can believe such a thing. He heard stories of lands where the hills were so steep and so high, they had snow on the top of them all year round and places that stretched on for thousands of miles, being made of nothing more than sand.

Thump! Thump!

Cragg jumped when, out of the blue, there came a bang at the inn's door. 'We're closed!' he said. He was surprised anyone would assume he'd still be open.

THUMP! THUMP! THUMP!

Whoever was outside clearly wasn't getting the message. 'Go home! It's Winter Festival Eve,' shouted Cragg.

BANG!

The door was struck a third time, so hard that it made the bottles and glasses rattle behind the bar. Cragg muttered angrily to himself, before climbing off his stool and shuffling over to see who it was. 'All rights, all rights!' he said. 'Keeps your blooming wig on.'

As he slid the bolts back on the door, it burst open and he was sent flying backwards across the room where he ended his journey crashing painfully into the bar. Duke squawked in anger and flapped his tatty old wings before running at the intruders, his claws and beak ready to inflict some serious damage. Before he knew what was happening, the bigger of the two men had kicked him like a raggedy feathered ball. It sent poor Duke flying across the room where he smashed into some bottles before disappearing behind the bar in a shower of glass.

Stars flashed before Cragg's eyes as he hurried to make sense of what had just happened.

'Doesn't feel too nice, does it?' said Spratt as he and Flob stood over him. 'I said I'd be back, and I do like to pride myself on being a man of my word.'

Cragg looked up, his face quickly turning from bewilderment to rage when he saw who it was, and what they had just done. 'Spratt?' he said, before he cried out, 'Duke!' He tried to get to his feet. 'What have you monsters done to him?'

With very little effort Cragg was swiftly knocked back down to the ground again as Flob punched him in the eye. Flob was about to hit him again when Spratt held out a hand to stop him. 'Wait,' he said. 'I have a much better idea.'

'You always do,' said Flob, sulking.

'That's because I haves the brains,' replied Spratt, clipping him around the ear.

'Tie him up,' said Spratt.

Cragg lay on the floor, ropes tied tightly around him. He was snapped back to reality when Spratt slapped him around the face. 'Wakey, wakey!' he said.

'You hurt my Duke,' Cragg managed to reply, tears stinging his eyes.

Spratt began to laugh. 'Surely, you're not talking about that scrawny Winter Festival turkey, are you?' he said.

'He's a cockerel and he's a better being than you'll ever be, you horrible little man,' snapped back Cragg, trying to break free of the ropes but to no avail.

Flob laughed. 'He's funny,' he said.

'Shut up, you idiot,' snapped Spratt.

Spratt crouched down so that his face was almost touching Cragg's. 'Nobody ever calls me little,' he hissed through gritted rotten teeth.

'Not to your face,' replied Cragg.

Spratt's nostrils flared, and he stood back up. 'Knock him out!' he barked at Flob. 'Let's see how cocky he is when he's rotting away in Choke Island Prison.'

Cragg felt the blood drain from his face. 'No!' he said. 'Not there, please.'

A wicked smirk spread across Spratt's face. 'Oh, that got your attention, did it? Well, it's too late,' he said. 'Knock him out.'

Flob looked around the room for a heavy blunt object and his eyes fixed upon the mantelpiece above the fireplace. As he grabbed the candlestick, it didn't budge but there came the grinding of gears that was all too familiar to Cragg. Cragg could do nothing but watch on helplessly.

Spratt and Flob took an instinctive step back as the dresser rumbled to one side, revealing the hidden wooden door behind it.

'It's nothing,' said Cragg, but from the panicked tone in his voice it was quite clear that it was obviously anything but.

'Quiet!' shouted Spratt, going over to the secret door. As he got closer to it, his eyes widened when he saw the carving on the door. 'The Society symbol,' he hissed. 'Well, well, well, so that's where they've been hiding, is it?'

'I can explain,' said Cragg.

Just as Spratt was about to reply, there came a loud thump from behind Cragg and a scratching sound of claws on wood.

'Boss,' said an anxious Flob.

Spratt slowly turned around. The feathered creature stood on the counter of the bar and its scrawny neck popped and cracked as he bent it to the left and then to the right before its one remaining eye fixed itself on Spratt and Flob with a piercing stare. He then scraped his long claws on the counter like a raging bull ready to charge.

'Good boy! There, there, don't move. There's a good turkey,' said Spratt as he and Flob slowly backed away to the door that they'd barged in through just a little while earlier.

'He's a cockerel!' shouted Cragg. 'Get 'em Duke!'

Spratt and Flob screamed out as Duke let out an ear-piercing battle cry before he leapt off the counter and charged at them. Chaos then took over. Flob tried to take another kick at Duke but this time he was ready. He flapped his wings and flew over the

passing foot where he landed on top of Flob's head. Duke then dug his claws into Flob's scalp and held on tightly. Flob cried out in agony. He ran around the inn knocking over chairs and crashing into tables, while Duke pecked away at his forehead. 'GET 'IM OFF ME! GET 'IM OFF ME!' he shouted.

Spratt grabbed Duke's tail and tried his best to pull him off Flob's head, but all that happened was Duke dug his claws in even further. As Spratt wrestled with him, Flob's face was pulled taut over his lumpy skull so that his eyes bulged out of their sockets. 'LET HIM GO! LET HIM GO!' screeched Spratt. At just that moment, Duke let go of Flob's head. Spratt yelped as he was catapulted backwards flinging Duke over his head and sending him hurtling across the room. What Duke did next was rather surprising and somewhat impressive. While he flew through the air, he spun around and as he was about to hit the wall, he stretched out his legs. As they made contact, Duke squashed himself up before he sprung back, firing himself like a feathered missile at Flob and Spratt. They cried out in alarm as they were hit square on, sending them both crashing out of the inn, in a plume of feathers, onto the street outside. Hurriedly, they scrambled to their feet and started to run up the street with Duke in hot pursuit.

Meanwhile, Cragg was still lying tied up on the floor of his inn looking at the once hidden wooden door, open for the world to see, and he felt terror run down his spine. 'They'll tell! Whats 'ave I done. Stupid Cragg. Stupid, stupid, STUPID!' he said to himself, tears running down his face and getting himself into quite a state. He sniffed back the tears and his panic turned to anger, and it was what he needed to get himself motivated to fix the problem. He was The Society Guardian. It was his duty to protect The Society, whatever the cost. What had happened had happened and all he could do now was to do his best to make things right again.

'Sirs and madams, I won't let you down,' he said to the empty inn. With all his strength, Cragg managed to push himself up onto his feet. After a moment of getting his balance, he was able to hobble a few wobbly steps forward. Disaster then struck. As he took his next step, he tripped on an overturned chair. He watched the floor race towards his face. As he hit it, there was a sickening thud and he was instantly knocked out cold.

# CHAPTER 11

## *The Prime Minister*

As Spratt and Flob walked into the lavishly decorated office at the top of the Victoria Point Tower, it was fair to say they were scared. Before them, with her back turned, stood the tall, thin woman they had come to speak with. It took a truly terrifying person to frighten Spratt, but the person they were currently in the company of was one of them. Calmly, she continued to look out through the large round window, watching the snow fall outside. Spratt and Flob stood and waited. After some moments had passed, they both

wondered if she remembered they were even there. So, Spratt cleared his throat.

'Wait,' she said.

Spratt flinched. 'I'm sorry Prime Minister,' he said. 'It's just we have important…'

The Prime Minister raised one bony hand and Spratt knew from experience that simply meant 'shut up', which he dutifully did. Nobody else would dare tell him to do that, but the Prime Minister was the only person in Londonian Spratt truly respected. Her ruthless reputation was even more despicable than his and he admired her immensely for it. 'It is quite beautiful when the snow falls. I could stand and watch it for hours,' she said. 'Its delicate beauty is able to blind a person to quite how deadly it really is. Beauty can do that, you know?'

Spratt and Flob looked at one another and then back at the Prime Minister knowing that was very true. As she turned her head slightly to finally address her guests, her long, straight, raven black hair shimmered in the low light as it cascaded down her back like an inky waterfall.

'What is it you want?' she said.

Spratt and Flob were both still scratched, torn and covered in feathers from their encounter with Duke and when they both glanced at one another they hoped the other would speak first. Spratt felt the sweat run down his face.

'Well? You said it was important,' she said, turning around. 'Speak up. I won't bite.'

Spratt and Flob weren't completely convinced that was true.

'W-we have something to tell you, Prime Minister,' said Spratt, his voice barely a whisper.

'I think I have established that. What is it?'

After a few awkward moments of silence, the Prime Minister turned her back on them and spoke again, her breath creating a

white circle of steam on the large round window. 'I'm waiting,' she said.

'We've found them, Prime Minister,' said Spratt.

'Found who?'

'Them people you've been searching for, for a very long time, Prime Minister,' said Flob.

'What people?'

'What my colleague is trying to tell you Prime Minister is that we've located The Society,' said Spratt, his heart thumping painfully in his chest as he knew the enormity of what he'd just said. Spratt and Flob instantly looked down the moment the Prime Minister spun around to face them, her eyes boring into them.

'What did you just say?' she demanded.

'We know where The Society are Prime Minister,' repeated

Spratt.

She then almost seemed to glide around her desk, like a snake hunting its prey, before stopping just in front of them. Neither of them dared to move.

'You two have found The Society?' she said with a tone to her voice that was clear that she didn't believe them. 'You're lying to me.'

Flob and Spratt looked nervous. 'No! It's true Prime Minister. We found the entrance to their hideaway,' said Spratt, knowing that every word he spoke could literally be a life or death situation.

The Prime Minister said nothing for what seemed like an eternity before finally she spoke. 'My best men and women have searched for years trying to locate them but have turned up nothing. Then you two come walking in here looking like a couple of deranged bird nests and tell me you have found them?' she said. 'If you are lying to me, which I suspect you are, well I don't need to warn you about the consequences do I?'

Spratt and Flob gulped. 'Yes, Prime Minister,' they said.

'Are they aware you know of their whereabouts?'

'No, Prime Minister. Only the inn owner knows,' said Spratt.

'Inn owner?'

'He owns the flea pit inn where the secret door is,' said Spratt.

'They're hiding in an inn?'

'Yes, Prime Minister,' said Spratt.

'And what of the owner?' she asked.

'Oh, we tied him up good and proper,' said Flob, boastfully. His smile soon left his face when the Prime Minister stared at him coldly before she turned her attention back to Spratt.

'Gather together my best Guards. We're about to pay The Society a visit,' she said.

# CHAPTER 12
## *An Evening of Incredible Stories*

The golden quill had spun many more times over the remaining evening. The Society members had talked openly about The Other Lands and Arthur had sat listening to them, enthralled.

Mr Hardgrave had once again recounted a dark and unpleasant tale, but instead of a story about another murderous king, he had talked in rather graphic detail about a 'Dead Sea' where all that entered it died a horrible, salty death.

Madam Plummwith spoke of a strange plant that had a mouth that it used to eat insects with. Much to Arthur's delight, she had even brought a book along to show them what it looked like.

Lord Lurkybert was Arthur's favourite storyteller. Although his stories weren't always about The Other Lands, Arthur was still mesmerised by them. His tales were full of adventure and first-hand accounts about his journeys to the furthest reaches of Londonian, places many would never dare to go. He talked of the time he ventured into the Wailing Woods and how all the trees had been pulled over the years in the direction of The Storm. He was particularly animated when he explained how the sap had been drawn out of the trunks so that they created long golden coloured spikes jutting out of the sides of the trees.

Mr Quilymere's story had been about a funny looking animal that was a strange mix between a cat, a duck and an otter, if you can imagine such a thing. He did his best to explain it, but it was just so ridiculous, Arthur and the others couldn't stop laughing. Even Mr Quilymere himself joined in.

Arthur listened to everything The Society members had to say, soaking it all up like a sponge. The only person without anything to offer was Ida. When it was her turn, Mr Quilymere would jump in with another one of his stories which Arthur found rather peculiar. At one such interruption, Mr Quilymere talked of a place called Scotland.

'Where's that?' Arthur asked.

'Ah well, let me see. It is a place so very close to us and yet so very far, far away,' he replied. 'It's where my ancestors originally came from. A wonderful place found just beyond The Storm.'

'I'm still finding it hard to believe there is anything out there,' replied Arthur. 'At school, we were taught that there is nothing beyond The Storm.'

'It really is quite disgraceful,' said Mr Quilymere.

'At least you now know that it's not true,' said Ida, looking up and smiling at Arthur.

'School won't ever teach you the true nature of our world, Arthur. They're forbidden to. But, if you will let us, we will,' said Mr Quilymere. 'So, let us continue, shall we?' With that he pushed the button on his armrest and the quill once again retracted, spun around and pointed at yet another Society member.

Everyone turned to Madam Plummwith. She drummed her fingers on her chair's armrest before finally coming to the decision to speak. 'For the benefit of Master Boil, I should like to tell the story of Miss Gwendoline Corbeau and her almost unbelievable rise to power,' she said.

Arthur looked puzzled. 'Who?' he said.

'You may know her better as the Prime Minister.'

# CHAPTER 13
## *Gwendoline Corbeau*

'We know very little about the Prime Minister,' began Madam Plummwith. 'She may control, and be aware of, every aspect of our lives but we hardly know anything about hers.'

Arthur sat quietly and listened. The atmosphere in the room suddenly became much more serious.

'She has always been extremely protective of her privacy, Arthur,' Mr Quilymere added, 'which makes us all believe she has something important to hide.'

'Tobias is right but trying to find out what that is has been frustratingly difficult and dangerous. If anyone is ever caught asking questions about her, she thinks nothing of disposing of them. Tragically, The Society has learnt that lesson from bitter experience.'

Arthur felt very anxious. He looked around the room half expecting to see someone hiding in the shadows, silently listening in on their conversation.

Madam Plummwith straightened her wig and continued, 'Despite her best efforts, some bits of information have reached us over the years.'

Arthur sat forward in his chair waiting impatiently for what Madam Plummwith was about to say.

'The Prime Minister's full name is Gwendoline Corbeau,' she said. 'That much you now know. What you will not be aware of is that she was the daughter of a cobbler.'

Arthur's eyebrows raised in surprise. 'A cobbler? As in a man who mends shoes?' he said.

'Yes, exactly that.'

'But that's…'

'Citizens' work?' said Mr Quilymere.

'Well yes, it is, isn't it?' said Arthur. 'I always thought she was the daughter of a very powerful political family.'

'And that is exactly what she wants you to believe,' continued Mr Quilymere. 'The truth is our Prime Minister, a person that holds herself in the highest esteem, is nothing more than the daughter of a painfully ordinary working-class family.'

'And what is wrong with that?' said Arthur, sounding a little defensive given his own background.

'Nothing at all, of course, but it does make her rise to power all the more intriguing.'

Arthur thought for a moment, and then something dawned on him, something Madam Plummwith had said. 'You said she "was" the daughter of a cobbler. What happened to her parents?'

'Out of everything she has tried to hide in her past, this is the most troubling,' Madam Plummwith said. 'To answer that question, you must first understand that Mr and Mrs Corbeau worked for The Society.'

Arthur couldn't believe what he was hearing.

'They also knew, like we do, that there was a world beyond The Storm. That is why we know that the Prime Minister is lying when she tells the people of Londonian that there isn't.'

Arthur's brow furrowed. 'She's been telling everyone that there is nothing beyond The Storm and all the time she knows there is, why?'

'And there's the question we have been trying to answer since the day she came to power. How she went from being the daughter of a cobbler, a cobbler with connections to The Society of all things, to be the ruthless leader of The Collective. This is where we are at a loss too, Arthur. We've followed her rise through the ranks but what suddenly drove her to become the Prime Minister is still a mystery to us.'

Mr Quilymere then spoke, 'To answer your question about what happened to her parents, well, there's no easy way of saying this. She had them disposed of.'

Arthur gasped in horror. 'She KILLED her own PARENTS? That can't be true?'

'I'm afraid it is, my boy,' said Mr Quilymere.

'Quite the most wicked thing any human being can ever do,' said Lord Lurkybert.

'Sadly, it gets worse,' said Madam Plummwith.

'Worse?' gasped Arthur.

It was Mr Hardgrave's turn to continue the story, 'She didn't have her parents killed straightaway. No, that would have been far too easy. Instead, for many days, she had them tortured so that they would reveal the whereabouts and the names of the members of The Society. Despite all the pain and suffering they went through, they never divulged a thing.'

Madam Plummwith wiped her eyes. 'Poor dears,' she said.

'As William just said Arthur, they tried to break Mr and Mrs Corbeau, but they would never have given in to her,' said Mr Quilymere. 'They loved their daughter, but the creature that had stood before them had long stopped being the kind, intelligent girl they had raised as a child.'

'I just don't get it though. What made her do that?' asked Arthur.

Mr Quilymere sighed, 'I guess there just comes a point in a person's life where they must forge their own path. For whatever reason, that was the path she chose.'

'But joining The Collective and then…'

'Killing her parents? Yes, I know, it would be impossible to comprehend if it were not true,' said Mr Quilymere. 'You must understand Arthur, we can't tell you more than that.'

'But why not?'

'Because there is nothing else to tell,' said Madam Plummwith.

'We have managed to gather some bits of information about her life, but some are just too well buried even for us to unearth,' said Mr Quilymere.

Arthur had always known the Prime Minister was bad, but what he had just heard made her even more terrible than he could ever have had imagined. He was now even more certain and determined to stop the Prime Minister and The Collective and destroy The Storm.

# CHAPTER 14
## *The Prime Minister's Carriage*

The Prime Minister's steam-powered carriage thundered through the winding cobbled streets of Londonian leaving a great plume of acrid, sooty smoke in its wake. Trailing behind it, riding atop penny farthings, were the Prime Minister's fiercely loyal and much feared mechanical Guards. They all wore identical black uniforms over their intricately mechanised bodies. They could almost have passed for human if it weren't for the roaring furnaces that lit up the cavity where their faces should have been. It was how they responded to every one of the Prime Minister's commands though that was both mysterious and terrifying.

Inside the carriage, the Prime Minister sat opposite Spratt and Flob, both of them too frightened to do or say anything. They knew that the Prime Minister could easily decide if they lived or died, and they both also knew that murdering and torturing people was one of her favourite pastimes. Neither Spratt nor Flob wanted to speak first, but they were acutely aware that they had both been sat in silence for a very noticeable amount of time.

The Prime Minister gazed calmly out through the window as the streets thundered by. Spratt looked over at her. He really hoped that discovering the whereabouts of The Society was going to bring him some sort of financial reward. If he could only find a way of asking her. He glared at Flob and silently mouthed that he should say something first. Flob was stupid, but not that stupid. His eyes widened at the very idea and he shook his head. 'Coward,' Spratt muttered under his breath before he composed himself and cleared his throat. There was only going to be one way of knowing, he'd have to ask her himself. 'Prime Minister?' he said.

The Prime Minister looked over at him coolly. 'What?'

Spratt's mouth suddenly felt very dry. 'I was thinking. Seeing as myself and my… colleague here have found The Society and all, I was wondering if we may be in line for some… recompense?'

The Prime Minister, who had been staring blankly at him while showing no signs of emotion, raised a single thin eyebrow. This small gesture was all it took to shatter what little confidence Spratt had. And when Spratt got flustered, he was always in the habit of letting words come out of his mouth before he had a chance to really consider what he was saying. 'What I mean to say is, with The Society found and what have you, well, we…' he said.

'I heard what you said,' the Prime Minister replied, cutting him off. She then went quiet again and turned back to the window.

Spratt didn't know what to say so he looked angrily at Flob and prodded him in the side, before nodding at him to say something. 'You try,' he hissed.

Flob looked over at the Prime Minister and licked his lips. 'P-Prime Minister. Will we be getting a reward?' he said.

Spratt groaned. This time the Prime Minister spun around and her look was so piercing, Flob let out a little yelp.

'Are you telling me what to do?' she snapped at him, her eyes narrowing. 'Or maybe you are possibly trying to blackmail me?'

Flob and Spratt shook their heads vigorously and looked at each other panic-stricken. 'Oh, no, Madam Prime Minister! We weren't doing that, really we weren't,' said Spratt. 'We just thought that we'd done good and were merely giving you a suggestion on how to thank us.'

'Thank you?' said the Prime Minister.

'That's all right,' said Flob, grinning. Spratt elbowed him in the ribs. It took Flob a moment to realise why and he sheepishly looked down.

'You want ME to thank YOU?' she said again, her voice turning to a near whisper. There was no more a terrifying sound in all of

Londonian.

'No, no, not at all your Prime Ministerness,' said Spratt. 'It's an honour to work for you, it really is.' Spratt elbowed Flob again and he quickly nodded in agreement.

The Prime Minister eyed them suspiciously for what seemed like a very long time before she turned around and went back to looking

out of the carriage window. 'I need not inform you what will happen if you are not telling me the truth,' she said.

There was suddenly a blood-curdling howl from outside followed by a thud-thud-thud as someone rolled under the carriage and then along the cobbles behind it. Flob and Spratt gulped, but that moment of violence had put the Prime Minister in a good mood. The Prime Minister looked back at them. 'Being able to finally see the demise of The Society will be a fitting end to the year,' she said. 'Watching them be thrown into The Storm, along with all their destructive lies, will be cause for celebration. If you have found them then you will get your pathetic reward,' she said, and Spratt and Flob's faces lit up.

The Prime Minister stuck her head out of the carriage window and shouted up at the driver. 'Faster!' she said, making both Spratt and Flob jump. The driver nodded mechanically and pulled on a brass handle. There came a great roar as a shower of smoke and embers fired out of the back of the carriage shooting them forward into the blackness of the night.

# CHAPTER 15
## *Tied Up*

Pain flooded Cragg's whole body as he slowly came around and opened his eyes. Standing on his chest staring at him was Duke, his loyal feathered friend.

'Is that you, old friend?' croaked Cragg, staring bleary-eyed into Duke's gnarly face.

Duke pecked Cragg's nose and squawked at him. Cragg tried to move and he winced as the pain in his head pounded angrily. He struggled to sit up but found that he couldn't, and it was then that he remembered the ropes that Flob had tied him up with. Spratt and Flob. Despite the pain, his eyes suddenly shot across to the revealed secret door. 'Oh no!' he said, trying with all his might to break free from the ropes. Those two thugs would inform the Prime Minister of what they'd found, he was sure of it. He had no idea how long he had been unconscious for, but he could only hope it hadn't been long enough for them to reach the Prime Minister and tell her everything they knew. The Society needed to know they were in mortal danger and there was no time to spare. He had to break free from the ropes.

'Master Boil, sirs and madams,' he shouted out, 'Cragg will saves you!' He tried again to break free, but the ropes were too thick and too well bound. Cragg lay on his back and began to panic. He had to find a way to cut the ropes.

All the while Duke stood on his chest watching him with interest. Cragg glanced back up at him and it suddenly gave him an idea. It was crazy, but he was out of options. 'Duke. The ropes, can you peck me free?' he said. Duke tilted his head to one side with a look of confusion. 'The ropes. Can you peck the ropes with your beak?' said Cragg. 'You know, peck, peck, peck.' Duke stared down again and then jumped off Cragg and scuttled behind the bar.

All hope drained from Cragg and he let his head drop to the floor so that he now faced the damaged ceiling. It was a stupid idea and he felt daft for even thinking of it.

Scrit-scrit-scrit!

Out of Cragg's sight, he heard a funny sound. Before he could work out what it was, the ropes around him went slack and fell away. Cragg sat up in amazement, and when he peered down at the floor, there was Duke with a knife in his beak. Cragg gaped at Duke in surprise, but he had no time to thank him as Duke dropped the knife onto the floor before squawking loudly and flying straight through one of the unopened inn windows.

Cragg scrambled to his feet. There was no time to wonder where Duke had learnt to use a knife or why he had flown through the same window for the fourth time that year when there was a perfectly good door next to it. He had to get to The Society and warn them. He was about to go through the door when his blood ran cold. He could hear the unmistakable sound of a steam-powered carriage approaching.

# CHAPTER 16

## *The Prime Minister Arrives*

No sooner had Cragg locked the secret Society door behind him and the dresser moved back into place, the inn door burst open in a shower of wooden splinters. With a metallic whirr and the clacking of cogs and gears, two of the Prime Minister's Guards stomped in with their faces ablaze. They scoured the room for any sign of danger before one of them nodded giving the all clear. Ducking down as she entered, the Prime Minister regarded Cragg's inn with a look of deep disdain. She hated the Citizens. Everything about them disgusted her. They were weak and pathetic, and she only tolerated them because of their usefulness to her.

Spratt and Flob walked in warily, not wanting to come face to face with that deranged cockerel again, but, thankfully for them, Duke had long disappeared into the city.

The Prime Minister looked around the room. 'Well?' she said, fixing her eyes on them. 'Where is he and where's this door?'

Spratt's eyes dropped to the floor. His heart jumped in his chest on seeing the pile of discarded rope. Spratt punched Flob on the

arm. 'I thought you said you'd tied him up good and proper, you dim-wit!'

'I did!' Flob replied, rubbing his arm.

'Then how did he manage to escape?'

'Shut up!' snapped the Prime Minister, and both Flob and Spratt instantly did as they were told. Silently, she walked around the room before turning back to them.

'And the door?' she said, impatiently.

Flob stood with a blank expression on his face, before his brain engaged some moments later. 'Oh, right,' he said, going over to the fireplace where he pulled on the candlestick he'd grabbed earlier. Once again, the door revealed itself.

'Here it is Prime Minister,' he said, proudly, saluting for no apparent reason.

'Get out of my way, you imbecile,' the Prime Minister said, walking over and staring at the embossed symbol on the door. There it was, an inkpot with three quills in it. Slowly, her hand went

up to it and, with a bony finger, she traced along the indentations. Something quite unsettling then happened. The Prime Minister smiled. Turning her attention back to Spratt and Flob, they both took a step back. When the Prime Minister smiled, it usually meant she was about to do something despicable.

In spite of the possible danger they were now in, it didn't stop Spratt from remembering what he felt he was now due. 'Madam Prime Minister, seeing as you can now see that we were telling the truth and that we have found The Society, can we discuss our reward?'

The Prime Minister went silent, the smile leaving her face. 'Reward? How about I let you live for another day,' she said.

'But...' began Spratt but instantly stopped when the Prime Minister scowled at him.

'Need I remind you that you let this traitor escape,' she said, pointing down at the pile of rope on the floor, 'so, I would consider yourself lucky I don't have you executed for treason.'

Spratt gritted his teeth. 'Yes, Prime Minister,' he said. 'Most generous of you. But...' He was instantly cut off.

'If you say another word, I might have to reconsider my generous decision, is that understood?' she said.

Spratt snapped his mouth shut and felt the anger and disappointment boil away inside of him. 'Yes, Prime Minister,' he said.

'You're lucky I even want you around with your face looking like that,' she continued.

Spratt put a hand up to his sore nose. 'That was the boy's fault,' he muttered.

'What boy?' demanded the Prime Minister.

Spratt's nostrils flared at the memory. 'Boil. Arthur Boil. Son of Lily and Gerald. Nephew of Eliza Boil,' he said. 'He was outside here when that oaf, Cragg, hit me.'

'Here? What was he doing here?'

'Said he wanted to speak to Cragg about something.'

The Prime Minister's eyes narrowed. 'Where does this boy live?' she said.

'The old train yard. Eliza Boil owned it, but her sister and her pathetic excuse for a family live there now.'

'Owned?' said the Prime Minister.

'She was the Citizen that died in the hot air balloon accident, Prime Minister.'

For the briefest instance, the Prime Minister's face showed a flicker of concern. 'Yes, the accident,' she said. The room fell silent for a few agonising moments while Spratt and Flob waited to see what the Prime Minister was going to do next. 'Take six of my Guards and arrest the whole family, immediately. They will be joining these other traitors when I get my hands on them. They are involved in all of this too somehow.'

Swiftly, they left the inn, grateful to be leaving the Prime Minister to hunt down The Society with her remaining Guards, and allowing Spratt the opportunity he was looking for to get his revenge on Arthur.

# CHAPTER 17

## *A Bang on the Door*

Just as Mr Quilymere was about to start recounting another story, a loud bang came at the door making Arthur jump.

'Who's there?' demanded Mr Quilymere, getting to his feet.

'It's me, Mr Quilymere, sir,' Cragg gasped.

'Cragg?' Mr Quilymere said, worriedly.

'Open the door, Tobias,' said Madam Plummwith.

'Wait!' said Mr Hardgrave. 'How do we know it's not a trap? He shouldn't be down here for at least another four hours.'

'You daft old coot, nobody else knows we're down here,' said Lord Lurkybert. 'Open the door, old boy.'

Before anyone else could reply, Mr Quilymere went to the door and opened it. No sooner had the final bolt been slid to one side, then Cragg staggered into the room, his body drenched in sweat.

'Good heavens!' Madam Plummwith said when she saw how battered and bruised he was.

'Sirs, madams… trouble…' Cragg managed, just before he fell to his knees, completely out of breath.

'Quick, help me get the lad to a chair,' said Mr Quilymere.

Arthur and Lord Lurkybert got to their feet and together they hauled an exhausted Cragg over to Arthur's chair before placing him down in it. Madam Plummwith poured some water into a glass and passed it to him. 'Here, drink this,' she said.

Lord Lurkybert was livid. 'Tell me who did this to you. I'll give them a jolly good thrashing!'

After downing the glass of water in one gulp, Cragg looked up, fear clear in his eyes. 'No time… to explain,' he said, still trying to catch his breath.

Mr Quilymere put a hand on Cragg's shoulder. 'Deep breaths, my boy,' he said. Cragg did as he was told. He then sniffed loudly and tried again.

'I'm so sorry, Mr Quilymere, sir. One of them grabbed the candlestick and…'

'Who did?' asked Mr Quilymere.

'Spratt and Flob. Sirs and Madams, we must…'

'They saw the door?' interrupted Madam Plummwith.

Cragg looked into her eyes and nodded, tears flowing down his ruddy cheeks.

Mr Hardgrave gasped. 'Well that settles it, we're doomed,' he said, getting up and angrily walking over to Cragg. 'You had one job to do!'

Cragg put his head in his hands.

'Leave him alone!' snapped back Madam Plummwith.

'I will do no such thing! That buffoon has put us all in danger and…'

Arthur's attention was suddenly drawn to a distant sound. He could hear heavy footsteps echoing through the tunnels and that could only mean one thing. 'Listen!' Arthur said, and because of the urgency in his voice, the room fell silent.

'They're coming,' said Lord Lurkybert.

'Quick! Close the door!' said Mr Quilymere.

'But, we'll be trapped in here, you fool!' Mr Hardgrave said.

'Clearly it has skipped your memory of our current location?' said Mr Quilymere.

Mr Hardgrave looked at the table, then at Cragg, before looking back at Mr Quilymere again. 'You can't be serious?' Mr Hardgrave replied. 'We'll never all fit.'

'Never been more so, old chap,' replied Mr Quilymere.

Mr Hardgrave had nothing to add as Mr Quilymere hurried to the door, slammed it shut and pulled on a handle beside it. Numerous cogs turned, and metal bars shunted across in all directions locking them in. 'That'll keep them at bay for the time being,' Mr Quilymere said.

Only a few moments passed before there came a loud thud at the door making the chandelier swing back and forth. 'Open this door, immediately!' said the Prime Minster. 'I know you're in there.'

'We shall do no such thing!' Lord Lurkybert said. 'You want us then you are going to have to jolly well come and get us, you wicked, old crow.'

The Prime Minster roared out in anger. 'Guards, break it down, now!' There came the sound of many cogs and gears firing into action as the Guards hit the door again and again. The metal bars, that were keeping it in place, started to buckle.

Arthur watched as Mr Quilymere went to the table, grabbed the feather on the top of it and turned it one way then the other and then back again. There came a series of clicking sounds then a clonk. To Arthur's surprise the table rose upwards revealing a compartment beneath it, lit only by the glow of the green liquid that flowed along the table's gullies.

Ida looked on stunned, clearly as unaware of the hidden compartment's existence as Arthur was. 'What is it?' she asked.

There came another bang at the door and some of the cogs broke free from the locking mechanism and fell to the ground.

'It's a lift and we all need to get in it now before it's too late,' said Mr Quilymere.

Lord Lurkybert, with a great big grin on his face, walked over to it. 'Now, this is what I call an adventure!' he said, before climbing inside. 'Well, come on then you lot, unless you feel you can beat the Prime Minister and her band of tin cronies all on your own.'

Madam Plummwith climbed in, followed by Ida, Mr Hardgrave, Mr Quilymere and Arthur. The only person left to join them was Cragg. 'Come on, my boy!' ordered Mr Quilymere.

Cragg looked defeated. 'I'll never fits in there, Mr Quilymere, sir,' he said. 'Go on withouts me.'

'He's right. We'll just have to leave him,' said Mr Hardgrave.

'Nonsense! We'll do no such thing!' said Lord Lurkybert. 'We'll all just have to breathe in.'

There came another bang on the door.

'Barnabus Cragg! Get in now, that's an order!' said Mr Quilymere.

A metallic fist punched through the door and that was enough to get Cragg moving. Somehow, he forced his way into the lift, but everyone else could barely breathe. 'Hold on,' managed Mr Quilymere. He pushed a rivet on one of the lift's panels and they started to move downwards. Disaster then struck. The lift abruptly stopped leaving it visible in the Society room.

'That's not supposed to happen,' said Mr Quilymere.

'It's me, Mr Quilymere, sir! I is stuck.' said Cragg, quite panicked, his stomach hanging outside of the lift and preventing it from going down any further.

'Just suck it in lad!' said Lord Lurkybert.

Cragg took the deepest breath he could, and the lift began to groan and judder as his stomach slid against the wall.

That's it, lad! Don't breathe out, we're almost there,' said Mr Quilymere. 'Everyone, jump up and down.'

They all did as Mr Quilymere asked and, just as Cragg didn't think he could hold his breath any longer, the lift popped free. It was just in time too, for as the lift hurtled downwards and the last piece of the floor in The Society room slid back into place, the door burst open and the Prime Minister's Guards came charging in. They stopped then whirled around trying to find The Society.

As the Prime Minister walked in, her jubilant, smug expression was replaced with one of outright rage. 'Where are they?' she demanded. The Guards looked around and then back at the Prime Minister. Spinning around herself to scan the room, it was clear that they were nowhere to be seen. 'No, no, noooo!' she roared. The poor Guard beside her took the brunt of her anger. She picked it up off the floor and threw it across the room. As it slammed into one of the walls of artefact drawers, it shattered into a thousand springs, cogs and gears. 'FIND THEM!' she shouted.

# CHAPTER 18

## *The Rude Awakening*

With one swift movement Mrs Boil sat bolt upright, rolled out of bed and landed her bare feet straight onto the cold bedroom floor. The moment she'd heard the bang on the door, she knew it meant trouble. Quickly and quietly she went over to the window and peered outside.

'Oh, no!' she said to herself, hastily moving out of sight.

Silhouetted against the cold moonlight sky, with their metal faces ablaze, Mrs Boil saw six of the Prime Minister's Guards standing outside the train carriage accompanied by two men. Men, Mrs Boil knew all too well as Spratt and Flob.

'We have to get out of here,' she whispered, expecting Mr Boil to reply. Her lips pursed as she turned around and she saw her husband still curled up under the blankets, fast asleep, sucking his thumb. 'Get up you bloomin' Fopdoodle!' she hissed at him. He

stirred and grunted something unintelligible before rolling over, letting out an enormous trump and going back to sleep. Mrs Boil muttered something unsavoury under her breath, grabbed the cup of water on her bedside table and threw it over him. Before Mr Boil had a chance to cry out, she put a hand over his mouth. Looking back at her, with now wet bulging eyes, he watched as she brought a finger up to her lips. 'Not a word,' she whispered, before she removed her hand.

'What are you doing, woman?' he said, the volume of his voice putting a look of blind panic on his wife's face.

'Will you be quiet, you idiotic fool,' she fired back as she went over to the window and peered through it again. Luckily, it seemed their unwelcome guests hadn't heard. You want us to get caught?' she hissed, throwing her wet husband some dry clothes. 'They're outside now.'

'Who are?' said Mr Boil, quickly jumping out of bed and pulling on a pair of trousers. 'Is it the Gristle Brothers? Because I told them I'd pay them back on Tuesday.'

'No, it's not the Gristle Brothers,' said Mrs Boil, looking carefully out of the window again. 'You're going to wish it was though.'

'Lil, you're giving me the collywobbles. Who's out there?'

As if on cue, there came another loud bang on the door. 'By the command of the Prime Minister, I am ordering you to open this door!' screeched Spratt.

'Them,' said Mrs Boil.

'The Collective!' squeaked Mr Boil, his eyes widened in terror, all signs of sleepiness vanishing in a heartbeat. Now slightly hysterical, he tried to put on his remaining clothes as fast as he could.

'What did you do?' said Mrs Boil.

'I didn't do anything! Honest!'

'This isn't good. We need to get out of here,' said Mrs Boil.

'How exactly? They've blocked our escape route,' whimpered Mr Boil.

Mrs Boil gave him her usual look of disdain. 'You're a gutless coward, Gerald Boil, do you know that?' she said. 'What we are going to do is fight our way out.'

'Fight? B-but we have no weapons!' said Mr Boil.

A sly grin spread across Mrs Boil's face, a look that worried Mr Boil immensely. 'Well, it just shows how little you know. Luckily some of us are prepared,' she said. Before Mr Boil could reply, she had whipped off her nightdress. He looked on in horror, expecting to see his wife standing before him in nothing more than her unmentionables. Underneath though, Mrs Boil was dressed head to toe in what looked like a pair of men's breeches and a fencing jacket.

'What the Dickens are you wearing?' said Mr Boil.

'I may be a Boil by name, but I'm a Monroe by blood and us Monroes are always ready for action,' she said to her husband.

Mrs Boil went to the end of the bed, put her hand underneath it and pulled on a latch. The mattress sprung up and inside it was a secret compartment full of an assortment of weapons; pistols, sticks of dynamite and a giant club with metal studs on the end of it. 'Enough weapons for you, my dear?' she said to her stunned husband. She looked over the arsenal for a few contemplative moments before deciding on her weapon of choice. She lifted out the club, spinning it around a few times before smiling back at Mr Boil. 'If we're going to be smashing up tin men then you can't beat "Ol' Whacky",' she said.

Poor Mr Boil's brain had gone into a state of shock. He really had no idea what was happening or why. Without even realising he was doing it, he nodded back, now at a complete loss for words.

Another loud bang rang out through the carriage as the door to their home was hit again. 'Open up! I know you're in there,' screeched Spratt. Flanked by the six Guards and Flob, Spratt spoke again, 'I said, open this door!'

Mr Boil looked visibly terrified as Mrs Boil made her way to the door and then stopped. 'Arthur,' she said.

'I'll get him while you take care of that lot,' replied Mr Boil. Before Mrs Boil could answer, Mr Boil had seized the moment to make his escape. Mrs Boil muttered something rude under her breath.

'Have it your ways then, Boils!' screeched Spratt, gesturing for two of the Guards to come forward. 'Break it down,' he ordered. As they raised their metal fists ready to smash through the door, it burst open and Spratt was sent flying backwards. Mrs Boil jumped in the air before the two Guards even had a chance to react. She swung her club, hitting them both so hard their heads were knocked clean off their metallic shoulders. In a shower of black smoke and embers, their lifeless, headless bodies fell to the floor.

Before Flob could respond, Mrs Boil had managed to jump up into the air again and brought the club down on top of his head with a sickening thud. A stupid grin spread across his face as his eyes rolled up into his head before he toppled backwards.

Spratt looked up, his face and clothes now covered in sticky cold mud. 'Now you're in for it!' he said, before turning to the remaining Guards. 'Don't just stand there, you useless bucket of bolts, arrest her!' The remaining Guards fired up their furnaces and surrounded Mrs Boil on all sides. She could possibly handle two of them, but four was impossible.

Flob, coming back round, staggered to his feet and if looks could kill then Mrs Boil was very much a dead woman. 'I'm goin' to kill 'er!' he said.

Mrs Boil raised her club and prepared for battle. Spratt then stopped Flob. 'No, we have our orders,' he said. 'The Prime Minister wants the boy and she's going to tell us where he is, aren't you?'

Arthur? Mrs Boil thought, shocked and horrified to hear her son's name come out of that vile monster's mouth. What did the Prime Minister want with her son? She hoped Gerald had already managed to get Arthur away to safety. She may not be able to win against this lot, but she would still put up one hell of a fight. 'You leave my son alone. He's done nothing wrong.'

Spratt's face darkened. 'HE did THIS!' he said, pointing at his broken face.

'Arthur? Impossible.'

'Your son is nothing but a traitor. He's been colluding with The Society. Whom, I may add, will be meeting their end as we speak.'

Mrs Boil did her best to not show any emotion at what she had just been told, but inside her guts knotted. 'No idea what you're talking about,' she said.

'Tut-tut, now come on, we all know that's a lie,' said Spratt, grinning.

Mrs Boil desperately needed backup if she was going to have any chance of getting rid of these buffoons but when she looked behind her, she felt a sudden deep sense of betrayal. Her husband was nowhere to be seen. Just as she was about to do battle on her own, something quite unexpected happened. The window to the Boils' bedroom burst open and an unidentified object with a hissing fuse on one end came hurtling out of it. 'Get out of the way, Lil!' shouted Mr Boil as a stick of dynamite rolled to a stop at one of the Guard's metal feet.

Flob, Spratt and the Guards all looked at the object as Mrs Boil dived for cover. Before they could move, there was a great explosion and the train yard was showered in cogs, wheels and red-hot embers. Spratt and Flob were both blown off their feet and landed, with a giant gloopy splosh, in an enormous vat of tar.

'Are you okay?' said Mr Boil, running outside to join his wife.

Mrs Boil suddenly looked very worried. 'Where's Arthur?'

'I don't know. He wasn't in his room,' replied Mr Boil.

Mrs Boil then started to put the pieces together. The mysterious letter from her sister that the solicitor had given to Arthur, Spratt saying about his connection to The Society. 'Oh no,' she said, 'he's with the others and they're all in danger. We've got to help them.'

'The others?' said Mr Boil.

Before Mrs Boil could explain, there came a deep rumbling sound from above. Mr Boil looked up. 'What in the…?' he said.

Over the carriage, a giant object had appeared blocking out the moon and stars. Mrs Boil looked up too and watched as a rope ladder came tumbling down from above to land, fully unrolled, at her feet.

# CHAPTER 19

## *The Library*

After travelling downward, for what felt like forever, the cramped lift finally jolted to a stop.

In the now bitter cold, it was Mr Quilymere that broke the silence. 'C-Cragg, w-would y-you be so k-kind as to b-breathe in f-for a s-s-second, p-please' he said, through chattering teeth.

'Right you are Mr Quilymere, sir,' replied Cragg, who seemed to be the only one that didn't notice the cold. Cragg sucked in a lungful of air and, with quite a notable feat of dexterity, Mr Quilymere managed to reach past him and push a seemingly random stone on the wall. With the ding of a hidden bell, an iron door sprung open and The Society tumbled out landing heavily in a tangled heap onto a polished wooden floor.

'Good gracious!' said a richly eloquent but rather surprised voice.

A voice, Arthur didn't recognise. As he looked up, he saw a gentleman with a dark bushy beard and twirly moustache look back at him. He was sat wide-eyed at a wooden desk, piled high with reams upon reams of paper, holding in his right hand a most remarkable quill that was now poised mid-sentence.

'Well, don't just sit there, Charles. Help us up,' managed Mr Quilymere, finding it hard to speak from under all the bodies now piled on top of him.

'Oh right, yes of course,' Charles said, placing his quill on the desk before hurrying over to help untangle the mess of arms and legs before him.

'What's happened?' asked Charles.

'What we have all feared for a long time,' replied Madam Plummwith, smoothing down her dress and straightening her wig. 'She's found us.'

'Please tell me by "she" you don't mean... her?' asked Charles.

'I'm afraid so, old boy. The Prime Minister has finally discovered where we've been hiding out all these years,' said Lord Lurkybert, making Cragg look guiltily down at his feet.

'No, no, no!!' said Charles, pacing backwards and forwards while nervously stroking his beard. 'That's not good, not good at all.'

'No, it's not, but for the moment we are at least safe down here,' said Mr Quilymere. 'But we mustn't be complacent. It won't take her long to work out how we got away and then she'll come for us. We must make the most of what precious little time we have to get things in order and make our escape.'

'You want me to leave my library?' said Charles. 'B-but this is my home.'

'I know Charles and I'm sorry, but we all knew this day might come,' said Madam Plummwith. 'It's the reason we built the library in the manner we did after all.'

'What library?' asked Ida, as Arthur thought the same thing. 'And what is this place, Uncle Tobias?'

Mr Quilymere smiled back nervously. It was clear to Arthur, he didn't know what to say. Charles then noticed Ida and let out a little yelp of shock. 'What's she doing here?' he asked Mr Quilymere, pointing at her, horrified.

'My name is Ida, thank you,' she replied, curtly, not taking too kindly to being pointed at.

Charles chuckled nervously before he stepped in closer to Mr Quilymere so that he was the only one that could hear what he had to say next. 'You know she isn't supposed to be with you,' he whispered, although Arthur could hear every word he said.

'I'm well aware of that, Charles, but what else could we have done? It's not as if we could have left her up there for the Prime Minister to find, is it?' Mr Quilymere replied.

'And why exactly shouldn't I be here?' asked Ida, having crept up behind Charles without him realising and making him jump. 'And while we're at it, who exactly are you?'

Charles turned around and nervously wiped his hand on his waistcoat before he held it out for Ida to shake. 'The name's Charles,' he said. 'I'm one of the Curators of The Society Library.'

'Library?' asked Arthur this time, looking around the small room they were in. It was meticulously decorated, with a lovely warm open fire, but it was far from being a library. 'Doesn't a library need books?'

'That it does, Mister...' Charles stopped, a look of recognition crossing his face. 'Oh, my heavens! You're Eliza's nephew,' interrupted Charles. Before Arthur knew what was happening, Charles had grabbed his hand and was giving it a very vigorous shake. 'It's an honour to meet you, young man. I'm sorry it took me so long to recognise you, but with your sudden surprise entrance and all,' he said.

'Pleased to meet you too, Charles,' Arthur replied.

Charles' face then came over all sombre. 'I am deeply saddened to hear of your aunt's departure, Master Boil. A most terrible turn of events indeed.'

The room went quiet until Mr Hardgrave cleared his throat. 'Need I remind you that we are all in mortal danger and need to get a move on,' he said.

'Of course, quite right,' said Charles, taking a key from his waistcoat pocket and unlocking the giant, heavy oak door at the back of the room. 'You wanted to know where the Library was, Master Boil?' he said, pushing open the door.

Through the doorway, Arthur gazed upon a room that stunned him. The Society room had been one thing but what he now found himself looking at was something else entirely. The Library was as large, and as impressive, as The Great Cathedral of Londonian. Its grand intricate ceiling, that arched majestically overhead, glowed in the candlelight from the many chandeliers that hung from it. It wasn't just shelves of books he could see either, wherever Arthur looked there were thousands upon thousands of strange and intriguing items, all of them laid out impeccably. There were so many weird and wonderful things to behold that Arthur didn't know where to begin; wooden glass fronted cabinets that housed a menagerie of unrecognisable stuffed animals and skeletons; shelves upon shelves of glass bottles with strange and exotic things pickled inside them; exquisite paintings of fantastical lands housed in grand gilded frames; and so many other strange items that it was just too much for Arthur to take in.

On either side of the room, extending up to another floor, were two grand spiral staircases surrounded by even more bookcases full to bursting with books and parchments.

'Why didn't you tell me about this place, Uncle Tobias?' said Ida, who looked equally as astounded by the Library as Arthur.

'No time to explain now, I'm afraid,' he replied, before quickly changing the subject. 'We must grab what we can and get out of here. Cragg, I'm going to need your help.'

'Right you are, Mr Quilymere sir,' Cragg replied.

Cragg and The Society members disappeared further into the Library leaving Arthur and Ida alone to explore.

Arthur turned his attention to the most interesting of all the items on display. The one that took pride of place in the middle of the Library. Held in place by a beautifully carved wooden stand was a large ball as tall as he was. As he walked towards it, Ida joined him.

'What is it?' she asked.

Arthur shrugged his shoulders. 'I've no idea,' he said.

Ida gave the ball a push and it rotated around. 'Maybe The Society have told me about it before. If they have, I might have written it

down in my notebook,' Ida said, going to her pocket and retrieving it. After leafing through some of the pages she stopped. 'Here,' she said, looking over at Arthur.

Arthur moved in closer to look at the page Ida had stopped on. On it was a drawing that looked exactly like the ball in front of them and Ida had also scribbled down some notes beside it too. One area on the ball had been circled that read, 'You are here.'

'I wonder what that means?' said Arthur.

'Ah, I see the globe has caught your attention,' said Charles, walking back into the Library. 'Splendid isn't it?'

'What is it?' Arthur asked.

Charles chuckled. 'Now there's a question,' he said. 'So, have either of you ever wondered what lay beyond The Storm?' he said.

'Until today, I thought there wasn't anything,' Arthur said.

'Of course, The Nowhere. A nonsense story made up by The Collective. So, you have been informed by the others that there is a world beyond The Storm then?'

'Yes, they told me all about it.'

'And did they tell you about what The Other Lands actually looks like?'

'That there are strange animals and places there.'

'No, what I am talking about is what it really looks like?'

Arthur glanced over at Ida, both of them now confused.

'Sorry, let me make this clearer for you,' said Charles, putting a hand on the globe. 'This giant ball here is The Other Lands.'

Arthur and Ida must have looked very confused because Charles began to laugh. 'Sorry,' he said, once he eventually stopped laughing, but the grin on his face remained. 'I've seen that expression so many times over the years when I tell Society members for the first time that they actually live on the outside of a ball.'

Arthur looked at Charles to see if he was joking, but it was clear he wasn't. 'A ball?' said Arthur.

'That's impossible,' said Ida.

'I know, it's extraordinary, isn't it?'

'But, but we'd fall off it,' Arthur said.

'We would if gravity didn't make us stick to it. If we didn't have that, we'd float away,' Charles replied.

Arthur now felt quite unsteady on his feet. 'So, if I kept walking, I'd end up where I started?' he said.

'I haven't thought about that before, but I guess you would. Quite a long walk though,' replied Charles.

'What do you mean?' Arthur asked.

Charles rotated the globe and then stopped it. 'Here,' he said. Arthur and Ida looked closer at a small drawing of a swirling storm. 'That's Londonian right there. And this globe has been made to scale,' said Charles.

Arthur took a moment to process what he'd just been told, 'But it's so small.'

'Which makes The Other Lands incredibly big, doesn't it?' said Charles.

'Unfortunately, there is no time for me to tell you all about the wonders out there beyond The Storm but if you want to know more about the globe, or Earth as it's also known, then we have plenty of books upstairs you can look through while we get the boats ready,' said Charles.

Arthur looked at Ida puzzled. 'Boats?' he mouthed to her. Ida just shrugged her shoulders as they made their way to one of the spiral staircases.

# CHAPTER 20
## *A Book of Incredible Stories*

As Arthur and Ida wound their way up the staircase, Arthur gently ran his fingertips along the spines of the many old books on the shelves as he passed them. They may have become faded over the years and dog-eared from use, but Arthur knew that locked away between each of their covers there was something unimaginably wonderful to discover.

On reaching the top of the stairs, Arthur and Ida were met by a now familiar sight. From floor to ceiling, were many, many more books. Like children in a sweet shop, Arthur and Ida smiled at one another before running over to a different shelf to see what they could uncover about The Other Lands and the time before The Storm. Some of the books were partially burned which Arthur assumed were the ones rescued from the Great Burning. A particularly decorative book caught his eye and he reached for it. 'Oh wow!' he said, sliding it free from the shelf where its true splendour became evident. 'Look at this,' he said to Ida, holding it up for her to see.

She smiled back. 'Amazing,' she said, before she went back to looking through the books on the shelf she was at.

Arthur went over to a table and dropped the book down onto it with a dull thud. On the cover, lavishly decorated in gold and other precious stones, was the title of the book, 'The Thieves' Guild Handbook'. Handbook? thought Arthur. He could barely carry it. He began flicking through the pages and reading out extracts to Ida. 'Did you know there used to be a society of thieves?' he said.

'Did there?' replied Ida.

'They were called The Thieves' Guild and they were very powerful once.'

'What happened to them?'

Arthur quickly scanned through the pages. 'Here it is,' he said. 'It says that the Guild vanished when the members either joined The Collective or they were killed by them.'

Arthur read some more. 'It goes on to say that they used an intricate network of hidden tunnels to move around Londonian and stow away their stolen goods.'

'Like the ones to The Society Room? Does it say in that book where the tunnels were?' Ida replied, continuing to examine the books on the shelf in front of her.

'In the walls, apparently. It says that you can always find an entrance to the tunnel network at the end of a dead-end street.'

Ida turned to Arthur. 'What, all dead-end streets?'

'Not sure. Hang on.' Arthur read to himself for a few seconds more until he found the answer. 'Well, it says here that the street was always named after a flower. Something like Primrose Close, or Rose Square, that sort of thing.' Arthur turned to another page which had an illustration of two knives on it. 'And that on the brick wall, there would be one special brick with two daggers carved into it. To open the secret door, you just had to push that brick.'

While Arthur read on silently to himself, Ida returned her attention to the shelf in front of her. There were just so many books to choose from; books on ancient ruins, plants, animals, food, of kings and queens (whatever they were, she thought) and many other strange and unfamiliar things to her. One book intrigued her, its inviting golden title glittering in the candlelight. Ida slid the book free from the shelf and looked at the cover.

Unblinking she stared at the picture of a scared little girl wearing a blue shawl, running through a forest clutching a basket of apples as a monster chased her. Ida looked at the apples, and at the basket, and then at the monster and before she knew what was happening, she had let the book slip from her hands as a torrent of vivid memories washed over her mind.

Arthur, lifting his head to talk to Ida again, saw her start to sway

and rushed to catch her before she fell. 'Ida! Are you all right?' he said, helping her over to a chair.

'I - I remember!' she said, looking at him with a startled expression.

# CHAPTER 21
## *Ida Remembers*

'Something about what?' Arthur asked, worriedly. Whatever had just happened to Ida, he thought, it had clearly had quite a profound effect on her.

'Something… from my childhood… I think,' she managed.

Arthur didn't really know what to say, so he just squeezed her hand to comfort her. He'd had plenty of memories from his own childhood before, but none of them had ever made him faint.

'You don't understand, do you?' Ida replied, seeing the confused look on Arthur's face. She pulled her hand away from his. 'Has nobody told you?'

'Told me,' he asked, 'about what?'

Ida sighed, 'About, you know, my memory?'

Arthur shook his head again. 'Aunt Eliza never told me anything about anyone in The Society.'

'Then I guess you won't know that in just a few days' time, I may not remember any of this, even you.'

Arthur was stunned. 'What, nothing?' he said.

'Nothing,' Ida replied, the sadness clear in her voice. 'All I know about my life is what Uncle Tobias has told me and…,' she then took her notebook out of her pocket and held it up for Arthur to see, 'and what I write down in here.'

'But you've just remembered something though, haven't you?' Arthur said. 'Something from your childhood. What was it?'

Ida stood up and started pacing around the floor before she turned back to Arthur. 'This is going to sound crazy,' she said, 'I just remember a basket of apples. The picture in that book made me remember. They were bright red.'

'Were you carrying them?' Arthur asked.

Ida thought for a moment before replying. 'I was,' she said, and then added, 'there were lots of trees too. I was carrying them through a wood, I think.'

'Where were you taking them?'

Ida looked lost. 'I can't remember. I'm sorry, my head is such a jumbled mess,' she said.

'Just take your time. Take a deep breath and let the memories come to you,' said Arthur, trying to sound helpful. 'You said you were in a wood. Can you remember anything else about it?'

Ida closed her eyes and Arthur waited patiently. After a few moments had passed, Ida smiled. 'It was warm,' she said, opening her eyes and looking at him.

It was never warm in Londonian, Arthur thought, and he began to wonder if Ida's memories were nothing more than her imagination playing tricks on her. He didn't want to say anything though, as it was clear that she believed everything she was sayingw. Instead he encouraged her to continue. 'What were you wearing?' he said.

Ida's brow furrowed and then relaxed. 'A dress… with pretty yellow flowers on it,' she said, and then laughed out loud. Arthur could see that with the laughter came tears. Ida now looked scared and when she spoke again her voice trembled. 'There was a bright light,' she said. Her breathing quickened. 'It called my name.'

'What? The light did?'

'No,' she said, 'not the light. Something else.'

'What was it?' Arthur asked.

'I don't know,' replied Ida.

'Then try and describe it to me.'

'It… had wings where its arms should have been. It came towards me.'

Arthur was rapidly becoming concerned about Ida. The others were nowhere to be seen and there was only him to keep her company. The best thing he decided he could do to keep her calm was to keep her talking until Mr Quilymere, or one of the other Society members, returned. 'What did you do?' he asked.

'I ran as fast as I could.'

'And then what?'

'I fell.'

'Where did you fall?'

'Into a tunnel.'

'Was it a long tunnel?' he asked.

'I don't know… It was dark. It called out my name again and I ran.'

Arthur could see that Ida's memory was leading to something more troubling as she became much more agitated.

'Where did it go?' he asked.

'I don't know,' she replied. 'I kept on running in the darkness. It didn't follow me, but I was lost and so scared.' Tears were now flowing down Ida's face.

'How did you get out?' Arthur asked.

Ida closed her eyes. 'The light,' she said, and she hugged herself at the memory, rubbing the top of her left arm. 'I went towards it and… And, I didn't mean to and…' Before she could finish her sentence, Ida's eyes rolled up into her head and she fainted, slipping onto the floor before Arthur could stop her.

# CHAPTER 22
## *Discovery*

Another Guard flew across the room and shattered into hundreds of pieces as it hit the floor. It was clear The Society were nowhere

to be found in the room, but that didn't stop the Prime Minister, in her fit of rage, from taking it out on another of her Guards.

'Find them! Find them! FIND THEM!' she kept on screeching,

but they just stomped aimlessly around the room that was barely big enough to house them all in. After some time had passed and the Guards had explored every conceivable space, the Prime Minister had had enough. 'STOP!' she shouted, and all of her metal machines ground to a halt.

She crossed the room and stood where the table had been. 'Where are you?' she growled. In frustration, she stamped her foot on the floor and as she did so, it made a hollow thunk sound that made her look down. She did it again. 'They're under the floor,' she said, stepping to one side and pointing at the place where she'd just been standing. 'Tear it up.' With that, the Guards burst back into life and started pulling away at the floorboards with their mechanical claw-like hands. They made short work of the wood as each board popped and split its way free.

When they had finished, the Prime Minister stared down through the large hexagonal hole into the gloom below. A lift, she thought. A little part of her was secretly impressed, but that was short-lived by her unquenchable eagerness to go after The Society. 'You, you, you and you,' she said, pointing to four of her Guards. 'I need to go down there.' They bowed their metal heads and positioned themselves around the hole. There they locked their mechanical arms and fell forwards together. When they were all perfectly horizontal, with their metal feet pushing against the sides of the lift shaft, the Prime Minister stepped onto their backs.

'Go!' she commanded. The Guards started their descent down into the darkness below.

# CHAPTER 23

## *The Botanical Chamber*

Arthur crouched down beside Ida and tried to wake her, but this time there was no bringing her around. Panicked, and just as he was about to go and get help, Mr Quilymere appeared at the top of the stairs. 'Oh, my heavens,' he said.

'She just collapsed,' Arthur said as Mr Quilymere rushed over.

'It's okay, my boy. It's not your fault.' He then gently stroked his niece's face. 'Ida, it's me, Uncle Tobias,' he said. She groaned and slowly opened her eyes. Mr Quilymere let out a great sigh of relief. 'Thank the stars,' he said. 'Are you all right?'

'I think so,' she said. Her eyebrows then furrowed. 'Where am I?'

'You're still in the Library,' Arthur replied.

Ida continued to appear confused. 'Library? What library? Who are you?'

'Oh, not again,' said Mr Quilymere, his voice thick with anguish. 'When will this curse ever end?' He smiled back at Ida. 'It's okay, my dear. It's just your Uncle Tobias and Master Arthur Boil.'

'Arthur and Tobias,' Ida replied, although it was clear to Arthur those names meant nothing to her.

'Can you sit up?' Mr Quilymere asked her. Ida nodded. Arthur and Mr Quilymere helped her up. She looked around the room, a bewildered expression on her face. It was as if it was the first time she'd ever seen it.

'Has she lost her memory again?' whispered Arthur.

Mr Quilymere sighed and moved closer to Arthur so that Ida couldn't hear them. 'So, she told you, did she? I'm afraid to say that she does that a lot, my boy,' he said. 'Every so often she faints and then when she wakes up her memory has all but been wiped clean. It really is most tragic.'

'She said something strange to me. About a wood and a monster,' said Arthur.

Mr Quilymere's face became ashen. 'What else did she say to you?' he said.

'Only that she had remembered something about when she was younger. That she was carrying a basket of...'

'Apples?' said Mr Quilymere, ending Arthur's sentence.

'She's said that before?'

'Numerous times. Ends with a light in a tunnel, doesn't it?'

Arthur glanced over at Ida. 'Do you know what it means?'

'To some degree we do but this is not the time for explanations. I need your help. We need to hide everything in the Library before it's too late.'

*

As Arthur and Mr Quilymere talked, Cragg and the other Society members were being led down a stone corridor by Charles. They all knew where they were heading, apart from Cragg. He had heard stories about the Library over the years but having seen it for himself, it was really quite something. Where they were now off to though was quite a mystery to him.

Eventually, they stopped in front of a stone wall and Charles turned to them. 'You know the drill. Expect the heatwave.' He then went to his jacket pocket and retrieved a horseshoe magnet from it. After a few moments of Charles moving the magnet around the wall, Cragg could hear the grinding of metal, like a rusty bolt being forced opened. There then came a hiss of escaping air as the stone wall opened up on great iron hinges.

Cragg could hardly catch his breath as the blast of hot, damp air hit him in the face. 'Gordon Bennett!' he said, making Charles laugh.

'I did warn you,' he said. Charles fully opened the stone door and Cragg instantly forgot about the heat as he stood before an unbelievably incredible and mesmerizingly beautiful sight. 'Welcome to the Botanical Chamber,' Charles said.

Cragg's mouth dropped open. In all his years, he had never seen anything like it. Walking into the enormous cavern was like being transported to another world. 'Wow!' he said, for there was no other word that could better describe how overwhelming it was. Towering above them were many majestic trees, their canopies hanging overhead like a magnificent leafy ceiling. On the ground, giant multi-coloured leaves and flowers sprouted from every possible nook and cranny.

The Botanical Chamber wasn't just a home for plant life either. Flittering around in the air were many different species of butterfly and other exotic insects, some as big as dinner plates. It was impossible for Cragg to know exactly how big the cavern was because the undergrowth and giant trees dominated the surroundings and limited how far he could see, but he could tell it was vast. He glanced up and had to shield his eyes from the light.

'Mirrors,' said Charles. 'We guide the light down from above through thousands of hidden channels.'

'Amazing' Cragg said.

'It is, isn't it? We never need to water or feed anything in here too you know. It all takes care of itself. It's quite a marvel of nature.'

By the stone door, there rested a giant cow horn. Madam Plummwith picked it up, took a deep breath and blew into it. The trumpeting sound echoed through the trees. Cragg stared nervously over at Madam Plummwith. 'Don't worry, it's the only way to get his attention,' she said.

'Whose attention?' asked Cragg.

Before Madam Plummwith could answer, a bony, leathery gentleman with a long, grey, scraggly beard came bounding out of the undergrowth brandishing a giant hunting knife. Cragg cried out

in surprise.

Panting like an old dog on a hot summer's day, the bearded gentleman stood before them, eyeing them all suspiciously.

'Good evening, Charlie,' said Madam Plummwith, nonchalantly.

A grin spread across the feral gentleman's face as he finally twigged who was standing before him. 'By Jove! If it isn't Eudora Plummwith and her band of merry men. So sorry about that, old girl. A bit of the old cabin fever makes one forget one is human at times,' he said, putting his knife back into the holder strapped to his back. 'I lose track of reality down here you know. Anyway, it's good to see you all.' He then spat onto his hand and wiped it on his beard before holding it out for each of them to shake, which they all dutifully did (not that any of them wanted to of course).

Charles spoke up. 'Right, well, I'll leave you to explain everything to Charlie while I go back and get the others,' he said. Before anyone could reply, he had disappeared back through the stone door into the corridor.

Charlie's eyes narrowed. 'Explain what?' he said.

Lord Lurkybert stepped forward. 'We're in trouble, old chap,' he said.

'What sort of trouble?'

'The Prime Minister and her metal monsters are on their way,' said Madam Plummwith.

Charlie's face lost all its colour. 'Down here?' he said.

Lord Lurkybert nodded. 'I'm afraid so, old boy,' he said. 'Unfortunately, that's not our only concern. Ida is with us.'

Charlie seemed to stand a little taller somehow. 'Then we shall do what we can to fight them and protect her,' he said.

'Give the blighters what for, eh?' replied Lord Lurkybert, a wide grin spreading out from under his splendid moustache.

'Except we're not equipped to,' replied Madam Plummwith. 'Have you both forgotten that this is a place of research, not war.

We have no weapons.'

'Hah!' retorted Charlie. 'Who needs weapons when I have enough fire in my belly to take on a whole army of her stupid tin toys.'

'Don't be daft, you stupid, old fool,' said Mr Hardgrave. 'You'll get us all killed.'

'I blooming will not!'

Mr Hardgrave didn't feel the need to reply.

'What we need to do is get out of here and make our way to the surface so we can hide for a while,' said Madam Plummwith.

'Hide!' snorted Lord Lurkybert. 'Lurkyberts never hide, madam.'

'Then look at it as merely time for us to regroup, weigh up our options and plan our next move.'

Lord Lurkybert thought for a moment. 'A tactical manoeuvre, you say?'

'Exactly.'

'Then why didn't you just say so? Cunning and devious. Blooming marvellous!'

Charlie laughed with excitement and clapped his hands enthusiastically. 'Marvellous indeed!' he said.

*

There came a great clang of metal and a thud out in the entrance hall as the Prime Minister reached the bottom of the lift shaft. This was followed by the splintering of wood as her Guards broke through the ceiling of the lift destroying The Society's Dedication Table. Two pairs of metallic hands then grabbed the side of the iron door and forced it open.

For a woman so tall, the Prime Minister seemed to almost glide into the room as she ducked down to get through the doorway. She scanned the room, her eyes focusing on the desk Charles had been sat at earlier. She went over to it. Picking up one of the many pieces of paper he'd written on, she read, 'Beyond The Storm - A history of The Other Lands, by Charles D.' 'Treasonous scum,' she said, screwing up the sheet of paper and throwing it into the fire. 'Burn the rest of it,' she said to one of her Guards.

Her attention then turned to the great oak door at the back of the room. She went over to it and tried the handle finding, not to her surprise, that it was locked. 'Break it down,' she told the Guards that had piled down the lift shaft behind her.

*

On entering the Library, Charles was horrified to see that nothing had been packed away. He was then even more horrified when he saw Mr Quilymere and Arthur helping Ida down the stairs.

'What happened?' he said.

'No time to explain, old boy. We need to get Ida to safety with the others and then come back and pack up the Library,' said Mr Quilymere.

'I'll take her,' said Charles, 'while you pack everything away.'

Charles put his arm around Ida's waist and guided her to the corridor leading to the Botanical Chamber.

Arthur looked around the Library, full from floor to ceiling with hundreds, possibly thousands, of artefacts and he couldn't help thinking that there was an awful lot of things to pack away.

'I know what you're thinking, my boy,' said Mr Quilymere, reading Arthur's mind, 'where are we going to hide this lot? Luckily, we've already planned for just such a scenario.' Mr Quilymere pulled out a magnet from his pocket and went over to an engraving on the wall where he put the magnet against it. There was a clonk as the magnet appeared to attach to something. 'The trick,' he said to Arthur, moving the magnet along and then up, 'is to remember the shape of the bolt rail behind the wall.'

Arthur thought that was particularly clever, a locked door without a visible key.

Mr Quilymere moved the magnet down and to the right. On the last movement, there came a dull click and a big grin spread across Mr Quilymere's face as a little compartment opened revealing a metal lever behind it. 'Bingo!' he said. As he pulled on the lever, Arthur was amazed to see the Library displays, bookshelves and cabinets begin to move into hidden cavities within the walls and floors. Once the Library had emptied, the hidden cavities closed back up. The chandeliers were then hoisted upwards disappearing behind shutters which came across to conceal the entire ornate ceiling. Finally, all that was left were the two spiral staircases which, to Arthur's amazement, corkscrewed down into the ground.

BANG!

The impact on the giant oak door to the Library echoed off the now empty cavern. Arthur and Mr Quilymere exchanged worried looks. 'They've found us quicker than I dared hope,' said Mr Quilymere. 'We have to get out of here. That door is strong, but it won't hold the Prime Minister's Guards for long.'

Just to emphasise his point, the door was hit again, and a large crack appeared in the wood.

*

Charlie led Cragg, Madam Plummwith, Mr Hardgrave and Lord Lurkybert through the thick undergrowth, cutting a pathway with his giant hunting knife.

Cragg had never seen such a kaleidoscopic array of colour. He had become used to the angular dead greys and browns of the city. Out of everything he saw, it was the butterflies that he found to be the most mesmerising. They were so beautiful and so delicate. He held out a hand and one of them flittered down and landed on his plump outstretched finger. He went to touch it, but it took off into the air again. He watched with a big smile on his face as its brightly coloured wings gently flapped taking it high up into the canopy.

Every time Cragg breathed in, he took in a lungful of oxygen rich air filling him with the wonderful, heady feeling of happiness. He loved this place.

'Here we are,' said Charlie, placing his knife back into its holder and walking into a clearing. In front of him were two ancient boats sat on a swampy looking waterway. They were so old, rotten and covered in moss that Cragg was amazed they were still afloat. 'We'll use these to get out of here,' Charlie said. As he walked over and put a foot on the edge of one of them, a big chunk of it broke free and fell into the murky waters below. 'Oopsy,' he said.

'Oopsy?' said Mr Hardgrave. 'If you think for one moment, I'm getting in that... THING you must be madder than you look, and that's saying something.'

Charlie appeared visibly annoyed. 'It's because they haven't been used in years, that's all,' he said.

'I can see that.'

'You can always stay here and fight the Prime Minister on your own if you like? Keep them at bay while the rest of us escape,' said

Madam Plummwith, the sarcasm quite evident in her voice.

Mr Hardgrave grumbled something incoherent under his breath, crossed his arms and shut his mouth.

'Where are the other sirs and madams?' said Cragg. Just as he said this, Charles came through the undergrowth with Ida.

'Ida!' said Madam Plummwith when she saw Charles supporting her.

'Worry not Eudora, she's just had one of her funny spells.'

'Where's Tobias and Arthur, old chap?' Lord Lurkybert inquired.

'They're just concealing the Library. They'll be with us shortly,' said Charles.

*

BANG!

A big chunk of the door broke off and came crashing down onto the floor.

Arthur and Mr Quilymere quickly ran through the corridor to the stone door of the Botanical Chamber. Mr Quilymere pulled the magnet out of his pocket to unlock the door, but his shaking hands dropped it. He gave out a yelp of dismay as it bounced across the floor. 'Oh no!' he said.

BANG!

Arthur ran over to the magnet, scooped it up and threw it to Mr Quilymere who clumsily caught it. His hands still shaking, he placed the magnet to the wall and stopped. He turned and shot Arthur a look of panic. 'I-I can't remember the combination,' he said.

Beyond the corridor, there came another loud bang on the door. Arthur's mind ignited. Even in such a desperate situation as this, nothing excited him more than a problem to solve.

'I've opened this door hundreds of times before and, the one day I really need to, I can't remember the combination,' said Mr Quilymere.

That's it! Arthur thought. He walked over to the stone wall and looked closely at the surface. He turned to Mr Quilymere. 'Can I borrow your monocle, please?' he said.

Unsure why Arthur would need such a thing, but not feeling it was the time to argue, he passed it over to him. Arthur then held it up to his own eye and used it as a magnifying glass. Peering closer

at the surface, he could see the wear marks where the magnet had been used countless times before. 'Follow my finger,' Arthur said to Mr Quilymere, placing it on the wall and tracing where the wear marks were. To their relief, there was a loud clonking sound as the bolt released and the stone door swung open.

There came another bang on the Library door. Hurriedly, they made their way into the Botanical Chamber, bolting the door behind them.

\*

If they had been a moment longer then it would have been all over for Arthur and Mr Quilymere. For no sooner had the door closed, the door to the Library finally gave way and the Guards came pouring in, followed by the Prime Minister.

The dark, empty Library was illuminated by the glow of the Guards' furnaces. 'Find them!' she screeched. The Guards dutifully did as they were ordered, fanning out to search the cavern. After a short time, one of the Guards tooted like a steam train whistle, signalling they'd found something.

Surrounded by her Guards, the Prime Minister made her way down the corridor that led to the Botanical Chamber. When she came to a dead end, her eyes became wild and furious. 'What's the meaning of this? It's a dead end, you fools!' she said.

The Guards silently tilted their metal heads downward so that their faces illuminated the floor. In the thick layer of dirt, there was a series of footprints. The Prime Minister's eyes followed them all the way to the wall. 'Don't just stand there, break the wall down!' she shouted.

# CHAPTER 24
## *Cornered*

'Where am I?' Ida asked, peering at Madam Plummwith. 'Do I know you too?'

Madam Plummwith gave her a reassuring smile. 'I'm Madam Plummwith and you're in the Botanical Chamber. These other people with me are all your friends.'

'Friends?' Ida said, looking around at everyone, confused.

Arthur and Mr Quilymere suddenly burst through the undergrowth and into the clearing. 'We have to go now,' said Mr Quilymere, sounding quite out of breath.

Before anyone could reply, there came a large crashing noise that echoed around the Botanical Chamber.

*

'I know you're in here. Show yourselves!' shouted the Prime Minister.

'Quick, into the boats,' said Charlie.

Charlie and Charles jumped into the smaller boat at the front. 'Stay on the waterway. It will take you to the harbour,' said Charles as he and Charlie grabbed the oars and started rowing as fast as they could.

Arthur and the others began clambering into the bigger boat, the old rotten wood groaning and creaking. They all squashed themselves up until only Cragg was left to get on. As he went to step in the boat, Mr Hardgrave held out a hand to stop him.

'What in heavens name do you think you're doing, William?' said Mr Quilymere. 'Let the lad aboard this instance!'

'I will do no such thing. If he puts as much as a toe on this sorry excuse for a boat, it'll sink.'

Cragg spoke up. 'He's right Mr Quilymere, sir,' he said. 'I is too

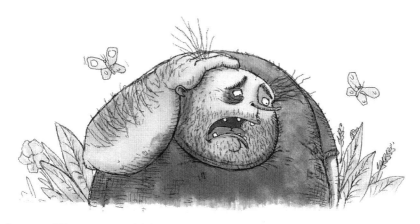

heavy. You go on without me. I'll hold them off to gives you a head start.'

'See! Cragg has the right idea. Now let's just get out of here while we can,' replied Mr Hardgrave.

Nobody moved.

'Come on! They'll be here any second.'

Lord Lurkybert sprang to his feet. 'A good captain never leaves a man behind,' he said.

'What the hell are you doing, you old fool?'

'If Cragg is courageous enough to stand up to those monsters then he can jolly well expect me to be by his side.' He then jumped off the boat and made his way over to Cragg.

Mr Hardgrave watched on in astonishment before turning to the others. 'We can still make it,' he said. 'The boat's a lot lighter now.'

'Will you just shut up, you self-centred halfwit,' said Madam Plummwith. She looked over at the others and silently they all came to the same decision. Together they stood up, climbed out of the boat and joined Cragg and Lord Lurkybert.

'This is ridiculous!' bellowed Mr Hardgrave, now sat on his own in the boat. 'You will all die. You know that, right?'

'Better to die a hero than to live as a coward,' snapped back Lord

Lurkybert.

'Well, I have no intention of dying.'

They all watched on in disbelief as Mr Hardgrave grabbed the oars and started to try and row away. Instead of being able to move it, the oars just awkwardly slapped the water with the boat barely

moving an inch. In a fit of rage, Mr Hardgrave eventually gave up. 'You idiots do realise we have no chance of winning, don't you?' he said, reluctantly clambering out of the boat and throwing the oars down on the ground. 'If anything happens to me, I will hold you all personally responsible.'

'You do that, William,' replied Mr Quilymere.

'Here they come!' said Cragg.

'I just want to say it's been an honour knowing you all,' said Lord Lurkybert.

In the surrounding undergrowth, they saw the plants and trees buckle and sway. The Prime Minister and her mini army of Guards were almost upon them. 'What do we do now?' said Arthur.

'We blooming well fight, laddie, that's what,' said Lord Lurkybert, grabbing a branch from the nearest tree and snapping it off ready to use it as a weapon. The others looked at one another and they knew that Lord Lurkybert was right.

A few moments later, the Prime Minister glided gracefully into the clearing.

'Keep back!' growled Lord Lurkybert.

She regarded The Society coolly and then tutted. 'Well, well, well. So, this is the infamous Society, is it?' she said. 'I can't say I'm impressed.'

'How dare you?' said Madam Plummwith.

The Prime Minister looked across at everyone until her eyes rested on Ida. The Society members swapped worried looks with one another. The Prime Minister stared at Ida and she stared back. When the Prime Minister's eyes narrowed, Mr Quilymere stepped between them. 'We might not look like much, but we have it where it counts!' he said, holding up a large stick in front of him.

'Put that thing down,' said the Prime Minister, focusing her attention on Mr Quilymere instead of Ida, 'you'll have someone's eye out with it.' The Prime Minister grinned at them. 'Well, I have to admit you've been a tricky bunch to catch. But, I'm a very patient woman and I knew you would slip up at some point.' The smile left her face, 'Now it's sadly over for you.'

Lord Lurkybert stepped forward. 'Never!' he said. 'You want us, then you can come and jolly well get us, you crazy, old crow.'

The Prime Minister's eye twitched, but the wickedly thin grin soon reappeared on her face. 'So be it,' she said, before adding, 'Guards!'

The Prime Minister's metal machines burst through the undergrowth and gathered around her. 'Arrest them!' she commanded. The first Guard headed straight towards Lord

Lurkybert. As it came at him, he jumped high into the air and swung the branch in his hands around. It caught the Guard on the side of the head. With a sound resembling a bell being struck, the Guard's head was sent spinning around on its pivot. With it now disorientated, and its head facing the wrong way, Cragg got together enough courage to run at the Guard, knocking it flying into the air. The Guard landed with a great crash onto the boat, breaking

it in half. The boat sank into the water. There came a loud hiss from the Guard's furnace as it was pulled down into the murky depths.

It was Lord Lurkybert's turn to grin. 'Got to try harder than that,' he said.

The Prime Minister's face contorted into a look of pure hate and rage. 'Treason!' she growled. 'I'll have you executed for that.'

'Well, that may be, but there's the small issue of arresting us first, Gwendoline,' said Mr Quilymere.

'What did you just call me?' replied the Prime Minister, stepping towards him. Mr Quilymere instinctively pushed Arthur and Ida behind him. He looked into the Prime Minister's eyes and stood his ground. 'That's your name, isn't it? Or would you prefer

Gwendoline Corbeau?'

The Prime Minister looked visibly rattled. The corner of her lip quivered. 'Nobody ever calls me that,' she sneered.

'Are you sure? Not even your late working-class cobbler parents? God rest their souls,' said Madam Plummwith.

The Prime Minister licked her lips and her eyes darted around nervously. Arthur noticed her hands were shaking. None of The Society had ever seen the Prime Minister like this before. 'LIES!' she said.

'It seems you are not as good at hiding the truth as you might think,' said Madam Plummwith.

'We shall see,' she snarled, before shouting, 'GUARDS!' again.

'Remember, knock them into the water,' said Mr Quilymere. 'We can stop them if we put out their furnaces.'

Another two Guards came at them. Madam Plummwith dived to one side as one of the Guards thundered at speed towards her. With a considerable amount of skill, she rolled over and grabbed one of the abandoned oars from the ground and used it to trip the Guard up. It flipped over into the air where it came down with an almighty splash into the water. There was another loud hiss as it too disappeared into the murkiness.

The second Guard charged at Mr Quilymere and Lord Lurkybert. Lord Lurkybert swung his branch again, but the Guard managed to move out of the way this time. As Mr Quilymere took aim with his stick, the Guard grabbed it with one of its metallic claws and snapped it in half. The Guard then turned its attention to Arthur and Ida. Arthur tried to push Ida behind him, but she refused to move. 'What are you doing?' she said, angrily.

'I'm trying to protect you,' he said.

'I can protect myself, thank you.' She then bent down, grabbed the other oar and ran at the Guard. The Guard skidded to a stop, completely taken aback by Ida's unexpected move. Arthur watched on in amazement. She jammed the oar into the ground in front of her and, like a pole-vaulter, she was sent flying into the air. She pushed her legs out in front of her just before hitting the Guard clean in the chest. It was sent flying backwards, its arms flaying around as it went straight into the water.

The Prime Minister screamed out in fury and ran at Ida. Just as she was about to crash into her, a rock came hurtling towards the Prime Minister and hit her hard on the cheek. She was sent stumbling backwards and she fell to the floor clutching her face.

When she peered at her shaking hand, she saw blood. She turned in the direction the rock had come from and she stared straight at Arthur.

Everything went silent.

'You,' she said, staggering to her feet, 'you did this to ME!'

Ida went and stood next to Arthur, brandishing the oar in front of her. 'Leave us alone,' she said.

The others regrouped and it was Mr Quilymere's turn to speak.

'It's over,' he said. 'Londonian will know everything there is to know about you, Gwendoline.'

The Prime Minister started to laugh, dark blood trickling down her cheek. 'You really think it was that easy?' she said. 'You think I'd let this opportunity go by and not come fully prepared?'

No one replied. The Prime Minister lifted both her hands over her head and clapped them together. Out of the undergrowth, a fresh legion of tin monsters appeared.

'Oh no,' said Madam Plummwith.

'So what? We can take them,' growled Lord Lurkybert.

Mr Quilymere sighed. 'I'm afraid not, old boy,' he said, dropping the remains of his stick onto the floor.

'I refuse to give up!' said Lord Lurkybert.

'We aren't,' said Madam Plummwith. 'We're buying ourselves time to concoct a battle plan.'

Arthur could tell that she didn't really believe that, but it was also clear that she didn't want Lord Lurkybert to feel his honour was being tarnished.

Mr Quilymere put a hand on Lord Lurkybert's shoulder and smiled at him. 'Eudora's right, old boy. We're not giving up quite yet,' he said. He leant in and whispered to him, 'But let's make the Prime Minister think we are.'

Lord Lurkybert grinned, fire reigniting behind his eyes. He then stepped gallantly forward and faced the Prime Minister. 'Drat! It looks as if you've got us after all,' he said, throwing down his weapon. He turned and winked at Mr Quilymere, who winked back.

'Guards, arrest them,' the Prime Minister ordered. She then touched the mark on her face and stared at Arthur. It was a look that made his blood run cold.

# CHAPTER 25
## *Choke Island Prison*

Arthur and The Society stood in the icy stone cell and shook uncontrollably. Arthur had never felt colder or more terrified in his entire life. The way the Prime Minister had looked at him was still etched in his mind. She had said he and the other Society members had committed treason and there was only one punishment for that. They were locked up in a place nobody in their right mind would ever want to find themselves in. A place where only the worst kind of Citizen was ever supposed to go, the infamous Choke Island Prison. It was hard for him to imagine a more terrible place to be, but he also knew from the stories that he had heard that it wouldn't be for very long.

Lord Lurkybert broke the silence. 'Right, let's hatch that plan to get out of here, shall we?' he said, turning to the others. 'Any ideas?'

'You really think there's a way out of this place, you old fool?' replied Mr Hardgrave. 'We are at the top of a tower, locked in a stone room with a thousand Guards between us and freedom. I'm sorry to break this to you Ernest, but we are not escaping from here any time soon.'

'Hah! Well that may be how you feel, old boy, but I for one refuse to give in,' said Lord Lurkybert. 'While I have breath in my body, I will fight on.'

'Well, I strongly suggest you stop wasting your time and give in to your fate.'

The only light, from a tiny barred window on one of the walls, illuminated Lord Lurkybert's face and Arthur could see that he bared his teeth at Mr Hardgrave but said nothing in response. Deep down it was clear to Arthur that even Lord Lurkybert knew the situation they were in was dire. Even if any of them could cut through the bars, which was quite unlikely considering they were made of solid iron and each of them over an inch thick, they would be met with a drop of several hundred metres. There was always the door into, and out of, the cell but that too was made of thick solid iron and bolted from the other side.

'I never tire of your overly optimistic view on life,' snapped Madam Plummwith, sarcastically, coming to Lord Lurkybert's defence. 'We'll get out of this somehow.'

'What is wrong with you lot? No, we will not. I may not be optimistic, but I am not delusional either. Nobody has ever escaped this place. We are not leaving Choke Island Prison, just accept it. And as we're on the subject of escaping, if it hadn't been for that great oaf over there, we wouldn't be here. So have a go at him, not me.'

Cragg sobbed uncontrollably as Mr Hardgrave pointed a finger at him.

'Leave him alone!' said Madam Plummwith, going over to Cragg, who was now sat on the floor, and putting an arm around his shoulder.

'I is so sorry Sirs and Madams, I have lets you all down,' said Cragg.

'Don't you ever say that. Nobody is to blame for our situation other than that monster of a Prime Minister.'

'Hear! Hear!' said Lord Lurkybert, before staring at Mr Hardgrave challenging him to disagree.

Nobody wanted to say it out loud, but they all believed that Mr Hardgrave was right about one thing. The situation they found themselves in was as bad as it got in Londonian.

They all fell silent, but it was hard to ignore the many other prisoners around them. Arthur noted that time and circumstance had cruelly turned each and every one of them into ragged, scrawny, pale versions of their former selves. They were either rocking back and forth mumbling to themselves or staring into space, having long lost the will to live. How long they had been there for was too much of a terrifying thought for him to contemplate.

Arthur looked over at Ida and saw she was shaking although she seemed not to notice. Her sad, unblinking eyes stared vacantly into the distance. Arthur took off his jacket and went over to her and placed it around her shoulders. 'Here, you're trembling,' he said.

Ida blinked and seemed to partly return to reality. 'Thank you…' she said, hesitating on the last word.

'Arthur. My name is Arthur.'

'That's right,' she said. 'Where are we now?'

Arthur thought about how to reply. Was it better she didn't know the truth? Instead, he said, 'Somewhere we'll be leaving very soon.'

'What happened to me?'

Arthur glanced over at Mr Quilymere to let him know that he would be best to answer that question. He came over, took hold of Ida's hands and looked her in the eyes. 'You fainted, sweetheart, and then you lost your memory.'

'Did I?' Ida said.

Before Mr Quilymere could continue, from out of the shadows, a squeaky voice spoke up. 'I knows that voice,' he said. A scraggly, nearly naked, bearded man got shakily to his bony legs and came tottering over to them. His eyes were wide and crazy, his face craggy and unkempt, and when he smiled it showed a row of blackened stumps where his teeth ought to have been.

Ida cried out in shock and Mr Quilymere jumped in between them. 'Keep back you scoundrel, otherwise I won't be responsible for my actions!' he said.

The man cowered back and licked his lips, his smile now leaving his face. 'I mean you no harm,' he said. He pointed a filthy talon-like finger at Ida. 'The young lady, who is she?'

'That's none of your ruddy business,' replied Mr Quilymere.

The man looked at Ida again. 'Who are you?' he asked. 'Your voice is familiar.'

Ida didn't reply.

The old man then clasped his filthy hand over his mouth and his eyes bulged in their sockets. He only removed it when he spoke again. 'Oh my, good gracious me. It can't be!' he said.

He tried to move closer to take a better look at Ida, but Mr Quilymere held out a hand to stop him. 'I said stay back,' he said.

The old man did as he was instructed but that didn't stop him from staring at Ida like he'd seen a ghost. 'Your name, it's Ida, isn't it?' he said.

Ida looked unsure if she should answer.

The man turned to the others. 'Her name is Ida, isn't it?' he asked.

'Shut up!' said Mr Quilymere, taking a threatening step towards the man. 'You don't have to tell him anything, Ida,' said Mr Quilymere.

The old man cried out in shock and stepped back. From behind him a pile of rags suddenly spoke, 'What are you making all that noise for, you daft ol' fool? I was sleeping.'

'It's her! It's her!' he replied, his voice getting higher and higher with every word.

'Who?!' shouted back the rags. 'You're making as much sense as old Gibbers over there.'

From a dark corner of the cell, a voice called out, 'Thank you!'

By now, every one of The Society members was looking at this strange, wizen old man and his pile of talking rags. 'The girl!' he replied.

'What girl?'

'You know, the GIRL!'

For some reason just by emphasising the word 'girl' more clearly, the top of the rags flipped back to reveal the shrunken head of a little old lady, as gummy and wide-eyed as the man. When she saw Ida, her eyes also widened in shock. 'Oh, my heavens!' she said.

'See, I told you,' replied the old man, grinning.

'But that's impossible,' she said, slowly getting to her feet and dragging the rags along with her as she approached Ida.

Mr Quilymere stepped in her way. 'You stay back too!' he said to her.

The old lady looked up at him and raised her eyebrows. 'Don't be such a nincompoop, Tobias. Really, you're as pompous now as you were as a wee lad,' she said. 'Now, move out of my way.'

Madam Plummwith chuckled and the old lady turned her attention to her. 'Something funny, Eudora Plummwith?' That shut her up. 'I didn't think so,' she said. 'Now, where is she?' She pushed a stunned Mr Quilymere to one side and shuffled over to Ida.

'Well, bless my soul!' she said, taking Ida's head in her hands. 'You're still so young but your hair, it's now so white. And your eyes too, why are they red? It is you, isn't it?' said the old lady.

Ida looked back at the old lady's face, confused.

'She doesn't remember you,' giggled the old man.

'Of course she doesn't, you daft old coot,' snapped back the old lady. 'It's been a while since we last met.'

Ida's confused expression stayed on her face. 'Who are you?' she asked.

'I think we would all like to know the answer to that question,' said Mr Quilymere.

'Oh, I'm sure you would, Toby,' she said. Mr Quilymere went quite red. 'Believe it or not, we used to play together when we were little girls?' she said.

That's impossible, thought Arthur. The old lady was probably a hundred years old but, as crazy as it sounded, nobody stopped to question her. Instead they said nothing and listened. Arthur noticed that Mr Quilymere kept looking over at Madam Plummwith, and she kept looking back at him.

'She won't remember you, my little pigeon dropping,' said the old man.

'Nonsense! She just needs a little bit of reminding, that's all,' the old lady replied. She then disappeared inside her rags, coming up a few moments later clutching a crumpled-up scrap of yellowing paper. 'Here! Look!' she said, shoving it at Ida. 'I kept it all these years.'

Ida looked at Mr Quilymere and he shrugged his shoulders. She turned back to the old lady and gingerly took the paper from her.

'Go on, open it,' she said with a toothless grin on her face.

Cautiously, Ida unfolded the paper. Inside was a drawing of a girl in her teens with dark, curly hair and a scar over one eye. She looked at the old lady and saw a scar above her eye. 'Aggie?' she said.

Aggie squealed with delight and grabbed Ida's hands before spinning her around and around. 'She remembers! She remembers!' she said, over and over again.

'See, my little pickled onion, I told you it was her!' said the old man.

As Aggie spun Ida around, a smile appeared on Ida's face. 'I do remember you!' she said to Aggie. 'I remember the trips to the market. How we used to play outside on the cobbled streets. We used to dance along to the street musician as he played on his barrel organ.'

Madam Plummwith had tears flowing down her cheeks, and Mr Quilymere wiped his away when he thought nobody else was watching.

Ida's smile then left her face and looked troubled. She let go of Aggie's hands and stepped back from her. 'But then you grew up,' said Ida. 'You got married to a man who made shoes for a living.'

'That's me!' said the old man.

Ida glanced over at him, now horrified to see how old both Aggie and her husband were. 'You had a daughter.'

Aggie sighed heavily and took a step towards Ida, but Ida stepped back from her. 'She had black hair... and so did I.'

'So, you do remember after all,' said Aggie, and sighed. 'I hoped you would be lucky enough to forget that much.'

Ida was lost for words. Madam Plummwith went over to her and held her close. She then turned to Aggie. 'Who are you?' she demanded.

The old lady sighed again. 'You might not like the answer to that question,' she said.

'Try us,' growled Mr Hardgrave.

'Ida always called me Aggie, but my real name is Agatha, and this is Jack, my husband,' she said. 'Or if you prefer, we are Mr and Mrs Corbeau.'

Madam Plummwith took a step back and looked as if she'd seen a ghost, which wasn't too far from the truth.

'But, that would make you…' said Mr Quilymere.

The old lady looked at them sadly, 'Yes, we are the Prime Minister's parents.'

# CHAPTER 26

## *The Corbeaus*

All the colour drained from Mr Quilymere's face. 'Mr and Mrs Corbeau?' he said. 'But you're supposed to be...'

'Dead?' said Aggie.

Mr Quilymere nodded, now quite unable to take his eyes off them. 'Well, yes,' he said.

'Then for two people that are supposed to be dead, we're rather alive, wouldn't you agree?' said Jack.

'But we heard such terrible stories about what had happened to you,' said Madam Plummwith. 'What your own daughter had done to you.'

'Of course you did. That was always her intention,' said Jack. 'She spread those rumours herself to make you believe we'd been killed.'

'She was amused by how much it would upset and frighten you,' added Aggie.

'What a horrible woman,' said Arthur, not being able to control his anger. He then saw the hurt expressions on the Corbeaus' faces and he felt guilty. They may have been the Prime Minister's parents, but it was clear they had as much control over their daughter as everyone else did. 'Sorry, I didn't mean to be rude,' he said.

'It's okay. We are well aware what our daughter is like. We are both as angry and as disappointed as you are,' said Jack.

Mr Hardgrave snorted. 'A daughter of two prominent Society members turning into that... creature,' he said. 'Disappointed? You should be ashamed of yourselves.'

'That's quite enough, Mr Hardgrave,' said Mr Quilymere, sternly.

'What for? For telling the truth?'

'This has nothing to do with how she was brought up. Jack and Aggie are decent people,' said Madam Plummwith.

Aggie turned to Mr Hardgrave, her eyes glistened as tears welled up in them. 'We loved our daughter very much,' she said, her voice breaking as Jack held her close.

'But we never raised her to be like this,' said Jack. 'Something happened to her that we just can't explain, and that's the truth.'

'Well, I believes you,' said Cragg. 'Me old dad thoughts the world of you, he did, and he was a very good judge of character. Said the Corbeaus were as decent a folk you would evers likely to meet.'

Mr Hardgrave huffed and crossed his arms, but he did nevertheless finally keep his opinions to himself.

'What do you think changed her?' asked Madam Plummwith.

'Well, we've always hoped Ida could help us with that question,' said Jack.

'Me?' Ida said, sitting down on an old stone bench.

Mr Quilymere stepped in, 'Completely out of the question. The poor lass can't even remember what happened yesterday, let alone that many years ago.'

'And have you even tried?' asked Aggie.

'We have tried everything we can think of,' said Mr Quilymere.

'Then you won't mind me having a go then, will you?' Aggie said, barging past Mr Quilymere and shuffling over to Ida where she sat down next to her. From the pile of rags that surrounded her, two hands appeared and reached out to Ida's. 'First things first, how much more can you remember?' Aggie asked.

Ida looked back, thinking. 'Nothing,' she said.

Aggie smiled. 'Well, I'm going to try and help you remember, if that's all right with you?'

Ida nodded.

'It seems that prompting your memory with words hasn't worked in the past. So, maybe we should try something else.' Aggie then disappeared back inside her rags and, after some rummaging around, she reappeared clutching an object in her hands. Ida stared at it confused.

Held out in front of her was an old wooden figurine. 'Here take it,' Aggie said, handing it to Ida. 'Do you know what it is?'

Ida turned it over in her hands. 'Gwenny?' she said, and a slight smile appeared on her face. Aggie beamed back clapping her hands in delight.

'Yes! That's right', she said.

'Should we be doing this?' Arthur said, remembering what had happened to Ida the last time she'd begun to remember things.

'As tough as this may be, my boy, I think we really have no choice but to try,' said Mr Quilymere. 'Aggie may be able to help Ida unlock some piece of information that could possibly help us all escape this dreadful place.'

'And what would that be exactly?' said Mr Hardgrave. 'Where the Guards put the key? The button for the secret door?'

'Well, it's the best option we have right now,' replied Mr Quilymere, 'unless, you have a better suggestion, that is?'

Mr Hardgrave's silence was proof enough to Arthur that he didn't.

Lost in thought, Ida ran her fingers over the carved face of the wooden figurine and stroked the pieces of thread that made up its long, black hair. 'She was my best friend,' she said.

Aggie squeezed Ida's hand as tears accompanied the smile on her face. 'Yes, she was,' she said.

Ida looked into Aggie's eyes, 'And so were you.'

Aggie chuckled, but Arthur could hear in that laugh that it was masking the pain she clearly felt inside. 'Yes, I was,' she said.

Arthur was confused. Did Aggie really just say that Ida played with her when they were both children? He stared at the wrinkled old lady in the ball of rags and then over at the fresh-faced young woman that was Ida. The time Aggie had spent in the cell had clearly affected her mind, he thought. Aggie was at least sixty years older than Ida.

Aggie grabbed Ida's free hand. 'Tell me a story about your time with Gwenny? You must have had lots of exciting adventures together?'

'We don't have time for this!' complained Mr Hardgrave.

'Will you just shut up, you miserable old windbag, and let Ida speak,' snapped back Madam Plummwith. Mr Hardgrave huffed, muttered something under his breath about everything being a waste of time, before walking away from the others and sulking on his own in the corner of the cell.

Ida glanced down at the figurine. 'I made this, didn't I?' she said.

'Yes, you did,' said Aggie. 'Do you know who it's a likeness of?'

Ida's brow furrowed. 'Your daughter,' she said. 'I used to play with her. We were best friends.'

Mr Quilymere looked over at Madam Plummwith.

'What happened to her, Ida?' Aggie asked.

Ida started to breathe much more heavily, and Arthur noticed the same look on her face that she'd had in the Library. She shook her head. 'No, I can't,' she said.

'Just go slowly and try your best,' Aggie replied.

Ida became much more agitated. 'I can't,' she said. 'Please.'

'It's okay, Ida,' Mr Quilymere said to her, before he turned to Aggie. 'That's enough,' he said.

Smiling kindly at Ida, Aggie took her hands in hers. 'You've done well,' she said, 'but I think we'll stop now.' Ida nodded and calmed down.

In his mind, Arthur tried to piece together everything he had heard about the Prime Minister. One thing puzzled him. 'Why did the Prime Minister not recognise Ida,' he asked.

'We don't know, Arthur,' said Mr Quilymere.

'She's changed from when Ida knew her as a child,' said Aggie.

'How did Gwendoline become the Prime Minister?' Arthur added.

'The truth is no one knows,' said Aggie. 'Nobody should be able to walk into The Collective's offices and demand to be Prime Minister, especially a young teenage girl. That would be impossible if it wasn't for the fact that she did just that.'

'It's obvious she had help somehow, but we have no idea who it was that helped her. No one does,' said Jack. 'For years, we've tried to uncover the truth, but many people have died trying.'

'If we can just find out who helped her then maybe it might give us a way to take that power from her,' said Arthur.

'Ida is our best hope,' said Aggie. 'Hopefully, in time, she'll be able to tell us what happened to Gwendoline.'

Arthur turned to Jack. 'How long have you been in this cell for?' he said.

'Long enough,' said Jack. 'She threw us in here decades ago. Way before you were even born.'

'Our own daughter just left us here to rot,' said Aggie.

'Well, she may not have had the nerve to dispose of you, but I can tell you now, she has no qualms about killing us,' said Mr Hardgrave. 'Your dear daughter is planning on executing us all tomorrow, if you didn't already know?'

'Of course we do,' snapped back Jack. 'We've had to watch many Society members spend their last night in this cell.'

'And you've never thought of helping any of them?'

'And how exactly would we do that? These walls are made of solid stone and are at least ten inches thick,' he replied, slapping the wall to make his point. 'After trying many times, you learn to accept the truth. There really is no escaping Choke Island Prison.'

Aggie sighed. 'I'm afraid he's right.'

'But we can't just sit here,' said Mr Quilymere.

'I'm sorry, but that really is all you can do for the moment,' said Aggie.

'Madam, I can assure you we will do no such thing!' said Lord Lurkybert. 'As long as I'm breathing, I will continue to keep fighting.'

From the far side of the cell, someone chuckled. 'You really think you have a chance of escaping?' the voice said, gruffly. 'We have watched the Prime Minister send hundreds of good brave folk, like yourselves, into The Storm. Of course, they try to find a way to escape but none have ever succeeded. So, if you want my opinion, accept it's over.'

The man who had just spoken was sat on the floor. It was impossible to see his face because of the thick layer of spider webs covering it.

'Well, where they have failed, we shall succeed, sir,' said Lord Lurkybert.

The old man turned his head slowly to look up at him sending

172

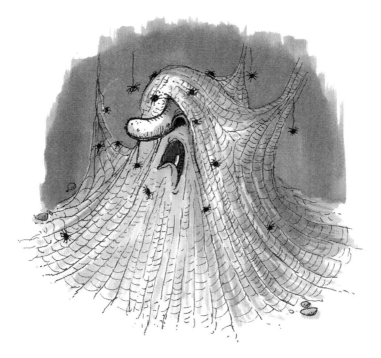

numerous spiders scurrying across his face and up into his wild, grey hair. 'That's what they all say,' he said. 'Cob's me name. I've been stuck in this wretched tower for over fifty years. I was once her top chef you know, until she threw me in here just because I didn't put salt in her soup. I ask you, fifty years for forgetting salt.'

Jack had clearly heard this story many, many times before because he was silently mouthing Cob's words as he said them. Jack was about to start talking when another voice spoke up from beside the barred window.

'Every year, I look out through this window and wish it was me out there being thrown into The Storm. Just think yourselves lucky your misery ends tomorrow,' he said. The man turned around. He had a striped face, having clearly stood in front of the barred window for too many years. 'The name's Finbar Thinwhistle, but you can call me Bars,' he said. 'I'd say it was a pleasure to meet you, but there is no pleasure to be had in here, only misery and

despair I'm afraid.'

Bars exhaled loudly, and the cell went quiet again. It seemed to Arthur that when either Cob or Bars had anything to say, this was going to be the usual response. They made Mr Hardgrave seem positively upbeat.

Looking over at the window, Arthur could see it was now snowing. He watched it tumble down from the night sky, the realisation about his fate suddenly hitting him. Instead of letting the fear consume him, he did what he had always done, he saw his situation as no more than a problem to be solved. He was a Monroe after all, and Monroes never, ever gave up.

# CHAPTER 27

## *The Last Morning*

The snow fell thick and heavy that night. Arthur looked out through the single barred window. He could just about make out the long execution bridge as it faded away into the blizzard and beyond. Arthur knew all too well what was to be found at the end of that bridge, and he also knew that he and the other Society members would shortly be led down it, never to return. He felt anger at the Prime Minister and her Collective cronies for putting them in this predicament and frustration for still not being able to come up with a way to get them out of this prison.

Everything that had happened to him over the past two days had happened so fast he hadn't had the time to process any of it, but during the night he had thought about nothing else. He wondered if his parents had noticed he wasn't even at home yet, and if they were now sick with worry. He kept thinking that if only he hadn't opened the letter from his Aunt Eliza then none of this would ever have happened in the first place. He tried to think of ways of escaping, but no solution presented itself to him. A painful knot twisted his insides. He sighed and turned around to face the others.

Aggie was still sat with Ida, both of them now wrapped up in her rags. Aggie had talked to Ida all through the night, telling her stories about their time growing up together and all about The Society. Arthur could now hear her telling Ida how when it became clear to everyone The Storm wasn't going to go away, a family of brothers, the Stones, had taken it upon themselves to start collecting stories and artefacts from The Other Lands.

'The Stone brothers opened a museum to house everything they could get their hands on,' said Aggie. 'They proudly called the museum "The Museum of Incredible Artefacts – Memories of

Earth." It was loved and visited often by the city folk. A beacon of hope that reminded people that one day The Storm would vanish, and they would be able to roam free again.'

'So, what happened?' Ida asked.

'The Collective. As is always the case with humanity, there are a few people desperate for control and power, having no qualms about taking advantage of a terrible situation to satisfy their desires. Politicians, gang leaders, corrupt businessmen; all of them decided to band together and create a new single rule of law. They wanted to turn Londonian into a place they controlled. To make sure nobody cared about anything or anywhere outside of Londonian, they brought about the destruction of everything that was known about The Other Lands.'

'The Great Burning,' said Arthur.

Aggie looked over at Arthur, impressed. 'Yes, exactly. The Stone brothers were obviously horrified, so they made a stand against The Collective by moving all of the museum's artefacts to a secret location underground, before going into hiding themselves, joined by a group of other like-minded individuals. This was the beginning of The Society. As soon as The Collective knew what they had done, they were furious, and they've been hunting The Society ever since.'

Aggie then looked very sad. 'Once upon a time, The Society had many members, but, as the years have gone by, those numbers have dwindled. Soon the people of Londonian started to forget about The Other Lands and believe what they were told. Time passed and a new generation of people emerged knowing nothing of a world ever existing beyond The Storm. It seems the longer a lie persists the more convincing it becomes. Those that were left of The Society were reduced to keeping the memory of The Other Lands alive by storing what artefacts still existed from it and educating one another on what they had learnt. All hope of ever removing

The Collective had gone.'

Listening in on the conversation, Mr Hardgrave turned to Aggie, 'Well, they've finally got rid of us completely now, haven't they?'

'Will you stop being so morose,' said Madam Plummwith. 'As usual, you're not exactly helping.'

Mr Hardgrave who'd been pacing up and down all night stopped dead in his tracks and spun around to face Madam Plummwith. 'Right, so sitting here and doing nothing is?'

'Pacing up and down like a caged crow is, I suppose?' Madam Plummwith snapped back.

Mr Hardgrave crossed his arms, huffed loudly and started pacing back and forth again.

Cragg had sat alone all night feeling desperately sorry for himself, muttering that the only place that was good enough for him was in The Storm. He felt he had failed in his duty to protect The Society and believed he had no way to make things right. No matter what anyone said to him, it made no difference.

'How many times do I have to tell you, none of this is your fault, my boy,' Mr Quilymere said, sitting himself down next to Cragg. 'You have been nothing but gallant in your duty to protect us, and you have been brave when bravery was called for.'

Cragg sniffed back his running nose. 'It's kind of you to says so sir, but I have to disagrees with you. I is a failure,' he said.

Lord Lurkybert had been pacing up and down all night too, but, unlike Mr Hardgrave, his steps were with a sense of optimistic urgency. He was certain there was a way out of the situation and, by Jove, he would figure it out. He'd asked Cob, Bars, Jack and Aggie many, many questions. 'How far down is the drop? How thick are the bars? How deeply are the bars embedded in the stone? How many Guards were there between the cell and the main prison gate?'

Arthur, now observing Lord Lurkybert, realised he too was trying to construct an escape plan. He had found a bit of old paper in his pocket, and with a pencil he managed to convince Ida to part with, he was furiously scribbling away. A smile began to grow under Lord Lurkybert's splendid moustache, but Arthur noticed it soon fade when it became apparent his plan wouldn't work. Intrigued Arthur went over to him. Maybe, he thought, if they put their heads together, they could work something out. 'Can I help?' he asked.

'I've looked at all the possibilities, laddie and I still can't find a way out of this ruddy hell hole.'

'Then let's work together,' Arthur said.

After some time swapping ideas and combining others, a plan began to take shape. 'And you think it will work, laddie?' Lord Lurkybert asked.

'It has to,' said Arthur, 'but it's risky.'

'Then it's a plan made for me, what?' grinned back Lord Lurkybert. 'Let's tell the others.'

Arthur and Lord Lurkybert went over to Mr Quilymere, Madam Plummwith, Jack and Aggie. 'We may have a way of escaping this infernal place,' Lord Lurkybert said, pushing the paper at Mr Quilymere and then tapping his finger on it.

Jack let out a sigh and looked at Lord Lurkybert. 'Ernest, I know you mean well, old boy, but this won't work,' he said, pushing the paper back.

'You haven't so much as given it a cursory look!' said Lord Lurkybert, sounding quite annoyed. He put the paper back in front of Jack.

'I don't need to, old chap. Over the years, I have seen every possible escape plan you can care to imagine. We've told you already, none have been successful.'

'None have been devised by a Monroe and Lurkybert though, have they?' said Lord Lurkybert.

'That's true,' said Jack.

'We all need to get out of here, including you too, Jack and Aggie,' said Arthur.

'The only way we'll fail is if we believe we have failed. Chin up, back straight and let's fight these blighters with everything we have. Agreed?' said Lord Lurkybert.

Everyone muttered in agreement.

'Good show! Right, let's take a look at the escape plan then, shall we?' he said. 'One hundred percent guaranteed to work. Trust me.'

They all silently looked at one another. Just as Lord Lurkybert was about to start talking again, there came a loud clanging sound at the door. They all got quickly to their feet and Aggie snatched the escape plan and hid it inside her rags. As the door swung open, The Society instinctively moved closer to one another. Filling the doorway stood a gigantic man. Cragg took a step back. 'Oh no,' he said.

'Get out of my way, you fat lump,' said a squeaky, scratchy voice as the gigantic man was pushed aside.

Mr Quilymere's lip quivered. 'Spratt,' he said as if he were chewing on raw sewage.

Spratt strutted in. Where he and Flob had once had hair, they were now as bald as eggs. It did nothing to lessen Spratt's grotesque appearance.

'Well, well, well, look who we have here. Can't say I'm impressed,' he said.

'Try and come up with your own insults, you skinny, little runt. Your crazy boss has already used that one,' said Mr Hardgrave.
Spratt bounded over to him and whacked Mr Hardgrave on the side of the leg with the cane that he was holding, knocking him to the ground. He then placed the end of the cane under Mr Hardgrave's pointy chin and lifted it up so they faced one another. 'Talk to me like that again and I'll personally see to it you are boiled in oil before they throw you into The Storm,' he sneered,

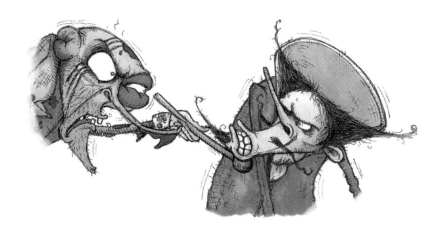

before whipping the cane away, letting Mr Hardgrave's head drop back down. 'Anyone else got anything they want to say?' continued Spratt. Flob cracked his knuckles.

'What IS that smell?' said Cragg, not being able to control himself any longer. 'It smells like tar.'

Spratt spun around and faced him. Cragg yelped. 'You trying to be funny?' he said.

Cragg vigorously shook his head.

It didn't matter how much Spratt and Flob had tried to scrub themselves clean after being blown into the vat of tar at the Boils' train yard, they just couldn't get rid of the smell. If Spratt got his hands on Mr and Mrs Boil again, he would make them pay for what they'd done. Nobody disrespected Spratt, ever.

Arthur and the others went quiet. Even Lord Lurkybert decided to keep his mouth shut on this particular occasion.

Spratt slowly walked over to Cragg. Cragg didn't dare move. Spratt peered up at him, a rotten toothy grin creasing his face. 'I think a lumbering, stupid, great oaf like you needs to be given the responsibility that best suits him,' he said.

Cragg looked over at Mr Quilymere and Madam Plummwith and they both stared back, not knowing what to say. They didn't know what Spratt was talking about either, but they were sure it wasn't going to be pleasant.

Flob, who'd been stood blocking the doorway, walked into the cell followed by five of the Prime Minister's Guards.

'Take them away,' Spratt ordered.

The usual confrontational Lord Lurkybert just turned and winked at Aggie as he was led out of the cell.

When the Guards got to Cragg, Spratt put a hand out to stop them. 'Not him. I've got something special for him,' he said.

# CHAPTER 28
## *The Winter Festival*

Arthur shivered as he and the other Society members were led out into the bitter cold bleakness of the prison courtyard by Flob. There they were forced to trudge through the snow to a horse-drawn prison coach where Flob shoved them inside, locking the solid oak door behind them. They all huddled together to try to keep warm apart from Mr Hardgrave who stood alone looking out through the

iron bars. 'If you have a plan to get us out of this', he said, 'now might be a good time to hear it.'

Nobody replied.

'Come on, Ernest! You said you had a way out of this,' Mr Hargrave said, turning on Lord Lurkybert.

'Dear fellow, we only had a plan for escaping the prison cell. I'm afraid one never anticipated this particular scenario,' he replied.

'Well, that's just great. Anyone else?'

Before anyone could reply, the large door across the prison courtyard was flung open and a giant man was violently shoved out into the open. He stumbled forward, falling to his knees onto the snowy ground and whimpered.

'Cragg!' gasped Madam Plummwith.

Poor Cragg's ankles and wrists were chained together and over his neck he wore, what looked like, a horse's collar and harness. The sadness in his eyes forced tears out of Madam Plummwith's. 'Oh, Cragg,' she said.

Spratt came strutting out behind him, now wearing a crumpled black suit and top hat. Lord Lurkybert was horrified the moment he saw what Spratt had clasped in his hands. 'That's a ruddy bullwhip,' he said. 'The scoundrel wouldn't dare?'

Spratt looked down at Cragg shaking uncontrollably on the ground. Spratt's split lip curled up in disgust. 'On your feet now, you pathetic halfwit!' He then pulled back his arm and cracked the whip right next to Cragg's ear making him flinch.

Madam Plummwith cried out in horror.

'I said, move!' Spratt growled.

Cragg did as he was told and scrambled to his feet. He shuffled

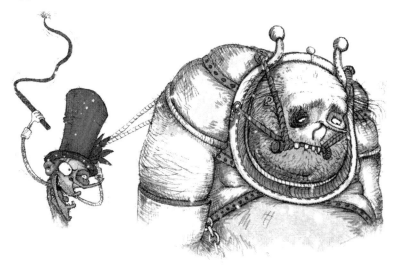

over to the prison coach where he was made to stand cowering in front of it.

'Leave him alone!' shouted Mr Quilymere.

Spratt grinned, turning to him. 'Now wouldn't that be a nice thing to do?' he said, sarcastically. He cracked the whip again and Cragg yelped. 'Get him ready,' he said, turning to Flob.

'My pleasure,' said Flob, coming forward and attaching Cragg to the prison coach as if he was the horse pulling it.

Beyond the courtyard, and in contrast to how he was feeling in the icy cold of the caged prison coach, Arthur could hear the distant muffled chorus of celebration. Music and laughter filling the air as people were enjoying themselves.

'Right you lot, be on your best behaviour,' said Spratt.

'Go to hell!' shouted back Mr Quilymere.

'Hell? Let me know what that's like won't you?' laughed Spratt. He nodded to the two Guards standing at the giant wooden gates on the other side of the courtyard. Their furnaced faces burst into life before they pulled across the thick wooden bar that held the gates firmly shut. Groaning and creaking the gates opened to reveal a walkway leading across an enormous stone bridge which faded down into the white, snowy abyss below.

That day, dancing and laughing upon the bridge, there were many thousands of Citizens. As the gates opened, they let out a great thunderous cheer. Arthur had never heard a more terrifying sound in all his life. Hate was one thing, but joyous bloodlust was something else entirely. Not only was everyone here to watch them die, they were there to enjoy it too.

The Citizens of Londonian had travelled from all over the city and the furthest reaches to stand on the bridge and witness the Londonian tradition called the 'Winter Festival Riddance'. It was a wonderfully jubilant occasion unless, of course, you happened to be the main attraction.

A great bell rang out sounding the beginning of the event and once again a great roar of excitement erupted from the crowd. A band started to play music as, with a crack of Spratt's whip, Arthur and The Society were pulled slowly outside by a very distraught Cragg.

When the crowd saw Cragg, they all started to point at him and laugh. 'Just ignore them, my boy,' shouted Mr Quilymere through the bars.

Inside the coach, Mr Quilymere turned to Arthur. 'This is how they have been brainwashed into behaving. Try not to judge them too harshly,' he said to him.

The Guards, who had opened the gates, now stomped along the bridge parting the crowd so there was a clear path. Behind them, a legion of more Guards followed stationing themselves along the bridge to keep back the crowd.

With Spratt leading the way and Flob following behind them, Cragg wailed out in sorrow as he continued to pull the coach. 'I is so, so sorry,' he kept saying. 'I has let you all down.'

'What are talking about, my good man? It ruddy well isn't your fault,' said Lord Lurkybert, peering through the bars at Cragg. 'Just walk as slowly as you can while we try and figure out a way to escape.'

Cragg nodded back, tears running down his face. Before he could speak, there came a crack of the whip.

'Move it, you great oaf!' shouted Spratt.

Cragg cried out in shock and pain.

'Leave him alone, you ghastly creature!' shouted Madam Plummwith, shaking her fist at Spratt.

Spratt cupped one of his ears with his free hand. 'What was that? You want me to whip him again?' said Spratt, grinning, before he cracked the whip at Cragg, catching him this time on the arm. Cragg shrieked out in pain as a nasty, red welt formed.

'Oops,' said Spratt.

'You will pay for this!' screamed Madam Plummwith. Before she could say anything else, Mr Quilymere had put his hand over her mouth and pulled her back from the bars. 'Get off me!' she shouted at him, shoving Mr Quilymere's hand away from her face.

'You're only making things worse, Eudora,' he said.

'Worse!' shouted back Madam Plummwith. 'How in heaven's name could things get any worse?'

'I'd rather not find out,' he replied. 'We need to spend what time we have left devising a way out of this.'

'Oh, will you just give it up,' said Mr Hardgrave. 'Don't you all think it's about time we stop pretending everything is going to work out?'

'Don't you dare,' threatened Mr Quilymere, rounding on Mr Hardgrave.

'Dare what?'

'Remove what little hope we have left to cling to,' he replied.

'Hope? You still don't get it, do you? Surely, even you can see that we have absolutely no way of getting out of this.'

Mr Quilymere stepped in closer to Mr Hardgrave, his eyes ablaze with fury. Mr Hardgrave took a step back and hit the back of the coach.

'Enough!' shouted Madam Plummwith.

Mr Quilymere stopped in his tracks, pointed his finger silently at Mr Hardgrave before turning around and walking back the other way.

'You think you're so clever, don't you?' said Madam Plummwith to Mr Hardgrave. 'Well, let me tell you something. If it's the cold hard truth you seem to enjoy so much, then chew on this. YOU are nothing more than a pathetic, failed magician. There, I've said it.'

A flicker of something appeared on his face Arthur had never seen before. He was sure it looked like hurt. As quickly as it had appeared though, it was replaced with his usual snide expression. 'Madam, being the greatest magician in the whole of Londonian is not what I would call a failure.'

'Well, then magic us out of here if you're so blooming fantastic,' replied Madam Plummwith.

'Okay then, I will,' he replied.

Madam Plummwith looked surprised as if she wasn't expecting that response at all. 'Well, good,' she said.

Mr Hardgrave stood at the back of the coach clearly at a loss at what to do next.

'Well, we're waiting,' said Madam Plummwith, crossing her arms, now the one with the smirk on her face.

'Seems the lady has you in a corner, old boy,' said Lord Lurkybert.

'A great magician needs time to prepare, that is all,' replied Mr Hardgrave, turning away and mumbling to himself.

'Well, you take as long as you like, my dear,' said Madam Plummwith, knowing she needn't hold her breath. She was just relieved he wasn't spouting out his usual hate-filled bile.

The coach continued to be pulled along the bridge. The crowd

booing and jeering while hurling bits of old food at it. Lord Lurkybert was bounding around challenging every Citizen who threw anything at him to a duel to the death. It amazed Arthur to see him in action. Even when all appeared lost, it didn't seem to dampen his will to keep on fighting. It was then, looking over at Ida and being spurred on by Lord Lurkybert, that Arthur decided to act. 'No,' he said, and The Society turned to him.

'No, what?' asked Mr Quilymere.

'No, we will not let those monsters win,' he said, feeling a power grow in him that was intoxicating. Arthur felt a hand slide into his and as he looked up, Ida smiled back at him.

'We fight them together,' she said.

Buoyed up by Ida's encouragement, Arthur looked at the rest of The Society. 'From what I have heard over the last two days, The Society are not cowards. Everything you have ever done was brave and courageous. You have fought back against The Collective for years and every time you have won. You have succeeded because you were never scared to fight back. So, let's fight back.'

'Count me in, my boy,' Mr Quilymere said, his voice choked up with emotion.

Madam Plummwith then grasped Mr Quilymere's hand and nodded in agreement. 'We do this together or not at all,' she said.

Lord Lurkybert let out a hearty 'Hear! Hear! 'That's the spirit laddie! We'll show the blighters, what for!' he said, before he charged up to the coach bars and stuck his head out through them, managing to just avoid a rotten cabbage as it was hurled his way. 'You hear that you scallywags! We are The Society and we are not afraid,' he shouted. A rotten tomato then came hurtling towards him and hit him smack in the face. He pulled his head sheepishly back through the bars and Arthur stifled a laugh.

'I believe a more measured approach is needed,' said Mr Quilymere, passing Lord Lurkybert his handkerchief.

The Storm wall was now becoming visible through the white fog. The terrifyingly gigantic, swirling clouds were a formidable sight. They thundered across the horizon, stretching as high and as wide as the eye could see. The wind too had picked up so that it howled loudly in everyone's ears and jostled the prison coach around making it even harder for Cragg to pull it.

Not even the icy cold or jeering crowds could dampen The Society's spirits any longer as they talked of a way to escape. Mr Hardgrave continued to stand at the back mumbling to himself. Arthur looked over to him muttering about how he WAS the greatest magician in Londonian over and over again. It was clear to Arthur that something more precious than Mr Hardgrave's life was at stake, and that was his reputation.

The coach reached the heavy, weathered timber platform at the end of the bridge. The crowd went silent. Arthur and The Society anxiously watched on as the doors to a hatch in the platform floor slid silently open.

# CHAPTER 29

## *The Show Goes On*

The hatch opened and hundreds of ravens flew out. As they dissipated to circle the sky, the Prime Minister magically materialised dressed head to toe in black ravens' feathers, her long, black hair dancing about her head in the howling wind. She glided

over to a podium on which a giant brass megaphone was mounted. The crowd roared with excitement until she raised a hand to silence them.

'My beloved Citizens,' she began, her voice echoing down the bridge carried along by the wind. 'Welcome to The Collective's one hundred and fifty-seventh Winter Festival Riddance.' The crowd erupted with cheers and clapping until the Prime Minister once again raised her hand to silence them. 'As you are all well aware, Londonian is a thriving metropolis of success, wealth and contentment.'

Mr Quilymere scoffed at that last word and the Prime Minister looked over at the cage, her eyes fixing on him.

'Sadly, there are some that feel the need to disagree.'

The crowd booed.

'She's lying to you!' shouted Arthur, and the crowd began to boo louder, throwing more rotten fruit and vegetables at the coach.

The Prime Minister raised a hand again and once more the crowd fell silent. 'So, it seems I am a liar,' the Prime Minister replied. 'Well, I'm sure everyone here would love to hear why. Bring the boy to me.'

She nodded to Flob who was stood by the prison coach. Arthur and the rest of The Society looked on horrified as he unlocked the door and he squeezed inside.

'Leave him alone!' shouted Ida, standing between herself and Arthur.

'You heard her, you great lumbering idiot,' said Lord Lurkybert, moving to stand next to Ida.

Mr Quilymere and Madam Plummwith joined them. 'If you want him then you are going to have to jolly well go through all of us,' said Madam Plummwith.

Flob looked on expressionless before he simply pushed them all to one side as if they were made of nothing more than paper. Before anybody could get to their feet, he grabbed Arthur by the wrist, dragged him outside and slammed the door shut and locked it again.

Madam Plummwith ran to the bars and watched on in horror. 'Arthur! No!'

'Bring him to me,' said the Prime Minister.

The Prime Minister stood to one side and gestured to the podium where the megaphone was mounted. 'Please, tell everyone what you know,' she said. Arthur didn't move. 'Go on, I won't bite,' said the Prime Minister, baring her teeth as she feigned a smile.

Arthur looked at the crowd who stood silently watching him, and then at the prison coach.

'Don't do it. It's a trap!' shouted Lord Lurkybert.

The Prime Minister spun around. 'Be quiet or I'll throw him into The Storm,' she snapped.

The Prime Minister turned back to Arthur and simpering said, 'Go on my dear. It seems only fair you get to tell your side of the story. I wouldn't want to seem cruel and unfair now, would I?'

Arthur looked at the podium again then slowly he began to walk towards it.

'No,' said Mr Quilymere, under his breath. 'Don't do it.'

Arthur reached the podium and stood looking out at the crowd. He glanced over at the coach again. Everyone inside was shaking their heads silently telling him 'no'.

'Go on, my dear,' the Prime Minister said. 'You may as well try and bring me down. That's what you want, isn't it? To humiliate me in front of the whole of Londonian.' She then walked around Arthur like a predator circling its prey.

'The woman you call your Prime Minister is a monster,' shouted Arthur through the megaphone.

The crowd gasped and went silent before they began to laugh.

The Prime Minister crossed her arms and smirked. 'Go on,' she said. 'We are all dying to hear what else you have to say. I know I can't wait.'

'You must all listen. She is lying to you,' continued Arthur. 'She never killed her parents. They are still alive and locked up in Choke Island Prison, in the same cell I have just come from.'

The crowd was now laughing so loud that Arthur was finding it hard to be heard. The Prime Minister played to the crowd. She leant in closer to Arthur and stuck out her bottom lip. 'I feel so terrible,' she said, mocking him. 'I really do.'

'Please! You must listen. There is a world out there beyond The Storm. A place with gigantic trees and rolling hills and animals as tall as the sky.'

A chant started from within the crowd. 'Throw him in! Throw him in!' over and over again until everyone was shouting it.

Arthur stood at the podium feeling completely helpless. 'Please,' he said one last time. 'You have to listen to me.'

The Prime Minister placed an arm around Arthur's shoulders. 'Well, I think we've heard enough, don't you? The crowd appear to be getting restless and I don't want to keep them waiting now, do I? Tie him up and place him on the catapult,' she said, gesturing to Flob who was stood by the steps to the platform.

The Society in the coach were beside themselves. They were now shouting for the Prime Minister to stop.

'Leave him alone!' shouted Ida.

'You harm just one hair on his head and so help me,' said Madam Plummwith.

'Keep quiet', said Spratt.

The only time the Prime Minister listened was when a voice suddenly came from the crowd. 'Stop that this instance, Gwendoline,' it said.

The Prime Minister spun around, her eyes open wide in shock. Before she had a chance to stop herself one word left her mouth, 'Mother?'

# CHAPTER 30

## *Ghosts of the Prime Minister's Past*

The crowd fell silent and parted to let Aggie and Jack through.
'You take that poor boy off that contraption right now!' shouted
Aggie.

The Prime Minister licked her lips and seemed to lose some of her
composure. 'H-how did you escape?' she stammered back.

'Never you mind that. What matters is that you put us in there.'
As Aggie and Jack shuffled towards the platform and passed the
prison coach, Spratt stepped forward to stop them.

'Leave it,' said the Prime Minister, 'I can take care of these two.'

'What has happened to you, Gwenny?' said Aggie.

'Your mother's right. We loved you and did everything we could
to make sure you had a happy upbringing. My Gwenny, how could
you have turned out like this? It breaks my heart.'

The crowd watched on silently. They had never seen anyone talk to the Prime Minister in that way before.

'Now, you listen here. You need to stop this charade this instance, and will you please let the people know the truth?' Aggie said. 'You know there's a world out there, beyond this stupid old Storm, so just say it.'

'Never,' whispered the Prime Minister, barely audible above The Storm. She then turned to address the crowd. 'Yes, these are my parents,' she said to them. The crowd began muttering among themselves. 'But pay no attention to them. I sadly had to put them both into prison for their own safety because they are both quite mad,' she said, pretending to wipe a tear from her eye. 'Don't listen

to a word they say. It's all absolute nonsense.'

'Gwendoline! How dare you speak to us like that?' said Aggie, starting towards the platform again.

'Throw them in the prison coach with the others,' said the Prime Minister to Flob. There was a gasp from the crowd as Flob stepped off the platform and picked both Aggie and Jack up. 'Get off me you dim-witted oaf!' shouted Aggie, punching and kicking him.

'See, completely mad,' said the Prime Minister to the crowd.

Flob carried Aggie and Jack over to the prison coach where he threw them in with The Society members. Before anyone could help them, both Aggie and Jack sprang to their feet and ran to the bars, absolutely furious. 'Let us out of here immediately,' shouted Aggie. 'Tell her Jack.'

'Let us out, Gwendoline,' he said.

The Prime Minister was done listening. 'Enough. Let's get on with the Riddance,' she announced.

Aggie turned to the others. 'I've seen our daughter do plenty of despicable things over the years and I won't tolerate it any longer,' she said.

Mr Quilymere and Madam Plummwith were still getting over the shock of seeing Aggie and Jack. 'You escaped but how?' said Mr Quilymere.

'All thanks to Arthur and Ernest's magnificent escape plan,' said Jack.

Lord Lurkybert puffed out his chest and his moustache twitched. 'I wish it could have been more refined, but I am glad it was sufficient enough for you to escape. The more pressing question is…'

'What are we going to do about Arthur?' finished Ida, looking out through the bars at him tied up in the giant wooden catapult.

# CHAPTER 31

## *From The Storm Came Fire*

BOOM!

With absolutely no warning at all, a bolt of lightning fired out from The Storm. Arthur looked up in surprise as it crackled and zigzagged across the sky, flew over his head and along the bridge before hitting one of the Prime Minister's Guards, obliterating it into a shower of sparks and mechanical parts.

'Hells bells! Something's happening to The Storm,' said Lord Lurkybert, sticking his head out through the bars of the prison coach and staring up at The Storm wall as more lightning snaked across its surface.

The Prime Minister looked curiously at the smouldering remains of the Guard before looking up at The Storm herself. As she did so, another bolt of lightning spat out from it. Somehow, she managed to duck just in time as it shot over her head and struck the bridge just missing the crowd. Panic stricken, the Citizens of Londonian started to run away.

'Stop!' the Prime Minister cried out, spinning around. 'I command you all to stop!' Nobody listened, the Citizens far too frightened to care what the Prime Minister wanted them to do. In all the chaos, a number of the Prime Minister's Guards, that were still obediently stationed along the bridge, were unceremoniously pushed off the sides as they tried in vain to stop the crowd from leaving.

'Don't just stand there you fools, do something!' the Prime Minister shouted at Flob and Spratt who had become frozen to the spot with fear. When another bolt of lightning fired from The Storm and struck the bridge right next to them, they both yelped. Without giving it another thought, and ignoring the Prime Minister's cries for them to stop, they joined the Citizens running away up the bridge and disappearing into the snowy blizzard.

'Treacherous cowards!' she screamed, her voice echoing along the now empty bridge.

'Gwendoline! Untie Arthur and get him down from that contraption immediately,' said Aggie from inside the coach. 'Enough is enough.'

The Prime Minister turned to her mother, her eyes wild and ablaze with hatred. 'Nobody tells me what to do!' she said.

The Society looked on in horror as the Prime Minister grabbed, with both hands, the catapult release handle beside her. 'I've waited far too long to get rid of you lot. I'm not waiting any longer.'

'No!' screamed out Madam Plummwith.

'Don't you dare!' shouted Aggie.

'What happened to you?' said Jack.

The Prime Minister's face dissolved into a wicked grin before she started to laugh. She then gripped the handle tightly again. 'I came to my senses,' she said, and before anyone could reply, she yanked back the handle.

The catapult slowly began to pull back into position. Arthur struggled with the ropes as more flashes of lightning lit up the inside of The Storm.

\*

'When that arm has fully retracted, she will only need to push that handle forward again for it to be released,' said Mr Quilymere to the others in the prison coach, now beside himself with worry.

'So, what are we going to do about it?' said Madam Plummwith.

'The Prime Minister is clearly not listening to reason.'

'We just need to escape from this infernal "cage",' said Lord Lurkybert.

'Then that is what we will do,' said a voice at the back of the coach.

'Well, that's so helpful of you, William,' snapped back Madam Plummwith at Mr Hardgrave. 'If you hadn't noticed we've been trying to do just that while you've been stood over there mumbling away to yourself.'

'Nobody can do that without a key. It's impossible,' said Jack, pulling on the locked coach door to make his point.

Mr Hardgrave raised an eyebrow. 'Impossible you say, sir?' he said, standing up tall and straight. 'Ladies and gentlemen!' he began.

'We don't have time for this,' hissed Madam Plummwith, but Mr Hardgrave ignored her.

'The Great Martini will now perform an escape of breathtaking brilliance,' he said, while dramatically removing his cloak with a theatrical twirl.

Mr Quilymere glanced nervously out to the catapult as it continued to be pulled down into position. He hated to admit it, but whatever Mr Hardgrave was up to, it was probably their last hope of saving Arthur.

'Not just any escape I hasten to add. On the contrary, ladies and gentlemen, this will be the greatest feat of escapology since magic began!' Mr Hardgrave paused for dramatic effect, as if waiting for a round of applause. He coughed when it was clear that none was forthcoming. 'I shall now call upon the great mystical powers of Hereshushu,' he said.

'Herry who?' said Lord Lurkybert.

'HERESHUSHU!' said Mr Hardgrave, relishing the attention he was now getting. Throwing his long, bony arms up into the air, he

wiggled his fingers in an over-exaggerated manner.

'GRANDMESIO METOETOE!' he bellowed, before throwing something down onto the floor where it burst into a plume of bright green, eggy smelling smoke. Everybody coughed and held their noses. When the smoke dispersed, nobody could believe what they were seeing. Standing on the other side of the locked door, holding a key in his hand, was Mr Hardgrave.

In spite of everything else that was going on, everyone's mouths dropped open in astonishment. 'That's impossible!' said Mr Quilymere. 'That's like…'

'Magic, my good man?' said Mr Hardgrave, unlocking the door.

'How?' managed Madam Plummwith.

'A great magician, madam,' Mr Hardgrave replied, 'never reveals his secrets.'

Everyone staggered out of the prison coach. The Prime Minister stared down at them in disbelief, a look that soon turned to rage. 'GET THEM!' she shouted to the few remaining Guards on the bridge.

Mr Hardgrave reached into his suit pocket and threw something onto the platform. The Prime Minister watched as it flew through the air to roll to a stop at her feet. Before she knew what was happening, it exploded in a great flash of light. 'You've blinded me!' screeched the Prime Minister, putting her hands over her eyes and staggering around the platform.

Ida didn't waste a moment. Before anyone could stop her, she made a run for Arthur. 'Don't Ida, it's too risky,' shouted Mr Quilymere, but she didn't listen.

'Let her go,' said Madam Plummwith. 'She knows what she's doing. The best thing we can do to help is to free Cragg and hold back the Guards.'

'Now you're speaking my language,' said Lord Lurkybert, rolling up his imaginary sleeves.

*

'Ida?' said Arthur as she reached him. 'What are you doing? You shouldn't be here. It's too dangerous.'

'You think I'm just going to leave you here? Let's get you out of this catapult before the Prime Minister gets her eyesight back,' she said, untying the ropes as quickly as she could.

The Prime Minister squinted in their direction. 'You!' she said, pointing a shaking finger at them both. 'I'm going to kill all of you!'

Instead of running, Ida stepped forward. 'You still don't recognise me, do you?' she said.

The Prime Minister faltered.

'What are you doing?' Arthur said. Ida took another step towards the Prime Minister. 'Go!' she said to Arthur, who was now free from the catapult.

'I'm not leaving you.'

Ida glanced at Arthur before turning back to the Prime Minister. 'Gwenny, it's me,' Ida said.

The Prime Minister's eyes narrowed. 'You call me that again and I'll kill you with my own bare hands,' she said. 'Nobody calls me that, ever!'

'I did once upon a time. Don't you recognise me? It's me, Ida.'

The Prime Minister hesitated, but then she shook her head and the hate-filled grimace reappeared on her face. 'I know exactly who you are, you're nobody,' she said. 'You're just pathetic city scum.'

Behind the Prime Minister, another flash of lightning lit up The Storm and this time Arthur saw something in it. 'Ida?' he said, but she wasn't listening. Instead, she took another tentative step closer to the Prime Minister.

'What happened to you?' Ida said.

'Stay back! You come any closer and I'll kill you…'

'With your bare hands, I know. We were the best of friends once,' said Ida.

This time the Prime Minister didn't move. 'Friends?' she said, looking directly at Ida with guarded curiosity.

'Yes, friends,' Ida said, moving closer to the Prime Minister. This time she didn't threaten Ida. 'We used to play together, you and I.'

A flicker of a smile appeared on the Prime Minister's face. 'We did?' she said, the venom in her voice gone as something seemed to register in her memory.

Ida reached out her hands to her, but as she did so, a terrible thing happened. A great fork of lightning burst from The Storm and hit the Prime Minister in the back. She screeched out in shock and pain as she was sent hurtling through the air and over the side of the platform. The blast sent Ida flying backwards where she hit Arthur, knocking them both to the ground.

Arthur was momentarily blinded. When his eyesight recovered, he looked at Ida. 'Are you all right?' he asked her.

'I'm fine,' she managed, 'but Gwenny, is she…?'

'Nobody could have survived that,' Arthur said.

'It wasn't her fault,' Ida replied, tears rolling down her cheeks. 'Something was controlling her.'

'Nobody controls me!' came a voice from behind them. They both turned around to see a black winged creature, with lightning coursing over its whole body, appear from beside the platform and hover in front of them.

Arthur and Ida looked on stunned. So, the wild rumours about the Prime Minister were true after all, Arthur thought.

'Gwenny!' Ida said, getting to her feet. She then took a step back as the Prime Minister's eyes met hers, all recognition now gone and replaced instead by only hate and madness. 'That pitiful creature is dead,' said the Prime Minister, 'and soon everyone related to her past will be too.'

She flew over to Ida and swatted her to one side, knocking her out as if she were nothing more than a fly.

'Ida!' Arthur said, but before he could go over to her, the Prime Minister landed on the platform in front of him. 'I am going to enjoy killing you nearly as much as I enjoyed killing your pathetic parents,' she said, a sadistic grin spreading across her face.

Arthur felt his blood instantly run cold. 'No, you're lying.'

The Prime Minister chuckled. 'I'm afraid I'm not,' she said, and Arthur felt the raw anger grow inside him. 'You should have heard them scream for mercy, quite pathetic.'

Arthur couldn't breathe. His parents. With everything that had been going on, he hadn't had any time to think about their safety, and now... Tears started to roll down his cheeks. 'I don't believe you,' said Arthur at barely a whisper, choking on his words and hoping beyond hope she was lying.

The Prime Minister started to laugh. Arthur's fists clenched tightly at his sides. He had never, ever considered killing anyone before. He knew it was the worst thing a person could do, yet, right at that moment, he thought of nothing else. He wanted to grab the Prime Minister and throw her into her stupid catapult before firing her into The Storm.

'Leave him alone, Gwenny,' said Ida, coming around and getting to her feet.

The Prime Minister spun around, her features contorting into fury as she bellowed, 'You just don't know when to quit do you?' Before Ida knew what was happening, the Prime Minister swooped down, grabbed her by her leg and carried her over to the catapult where she dropped her into the seat. Before she could escape, the Prime Minister fired electricity from her hands into Ida, stunning her.

Arthur couldn't hold in his emotions any longer. Roaring out with pure hate and desperation, he ran at the Prime Minister. As he leapt at her, she beat her wings and shot upwards, sending him tumbling heavily to the ground. The Prime Minister flew back down to the platform again and grabbed the catapult handle. 'Say goodbye to your little friend.' This time she pulled on the handle with all her might, snapping it off and throwing it to one side. The catapult arm sprung forward and Arthur watched on powerless to help as Ida was sent hurtling towards The Storm.

# CHAPTER 32
## *Reunion*

As the last Guard was thrown over the side of the bridge by Cragg, they all heard the twang of the catapult being released. Madam Plummwith looked at the body flying towards The Storm. 'Ida! No!', she cried.

'I can't watch,' Mr Quilymere said, turning away. Just as Ida was about to hit The Storm, a great flash of lightning surged across its surface as something burst through its wall. Whatever it was, it opened up and caught Ida, before snapping shut and retracting back into The Storm as abruptly as it had appeared.

The Society stood and stared, not knowing what else to do. The silence was only broken when they heard a cackling laugh. They all turned to see the Prime Minister, hovering in the air above the platform, surrounded by electricity.

'What in the blazes?' said Lord Lurkybert, gazing up at her.

'Murderer!' screamed Madam Plummwith, tears running down her cheeks.

'What have you done?' Aggie said.

'What should have been done long ago, old woman,' the Prime Minister said, floating back down to the platform. 'To rid Londonian of The Society once and for all. 'You can't beat me. You will die today and there is nothing you can do to stop it.'

Another great flash of lightning burst from within The Storm. It was so bright that it momentarily revealed a dark silhouette within it. 'What in Dicken's quill is that?' Lord Lurkybert said as a giant oval shaped object broke through The Storm wall in a great shower of sparks. 'Look!' A great toothy grin appeared from beneath his splendid moustache.

\*

It took Arthur only a split second to realise what it was too. He had seen that object countless times before and the moment he saw it, he had never felt such a powerful flood of emotions overwhelm him in all his life. He didn't know if he should burst into tears or jump for joy, or possibly both. An old train carriage, suspended under a large hot air balloon, manoeuvred itself overhead and came to a stop above the Prime Minister.

'No! No! Noooo!' screamed the Prime Minister, staring upwards. 'Impossible!'

A cannon appeared from under the carriage. Arthur recognised what it was and what was about to happen. With her back still turned, Arthur ran at the Prime Minister, leapt into the air and grabbed her ankles. The Prime Minister screeched out and tried to shake him off just as the cannon fired something large and round at her. Arthur let go just before the lump of sticky gloop hit the Prime Minister, knocking her out of the air and fixing her to the platform.

*

'Oh, my heavens,' said Madam Plummwith, as Arthur jumped down from the platform and ran over to them. 'Are you okay?'

'I'm fine,' he said, dusting himself down. 'Can't say the same for her majesty though.'

'Good work, laddie!' said Lord Lurkybert. 'Impressive manoeuvre indeed.'

The Prime Minister fought to free herself, but it was no use, she was stuck. It didn't prevent her from screaming one obscenity after another at Arthur and the others though.

'Look,' said Mr Quilymere, ignoring her and pointing at the airship. Leaning out of the airship's windows, and waving down to everyone, was Arthur's mother, father and Aunt Eliza. Arthur hadn't dared believe it, but now he saw his parents and Aunt Eliza with his own eyes, he couldn't stop himself and the tears flowed as he grinned back. A moment later, somebody else joined them.

'Ida!' called out Mr Quilymere.

'By jingo!' cried out Lord Lurkybert.

'Sirs and madams!' said Cragg, tears of joy filling his eyes. 'You is all alives!'

Mr Quilymere looked at the Prime Minister. 'It's over, Gwendoline,' he said.

A grin reappeared on the Prime Minister's face. 'You think a bit of tar is going to stop me?' she said, as the sound of metallic footsteps could be heard in the distance. Mr Quilymere turned his head in the direction of the sound. Appearing from the blizzard, and marching along the bridge, was a fresh wave of Guards hauling their own cannons behind them.

'You were saying?' the Prime Minister said, before screaming out, 'Shoot it down and finish this lot off.'

The Guards that were closest went for their weapons. Thankfully Eliza was one step ahead. Before they even had a chance to move, the cannon below the carriage rotated around and pointed directly at the oncoming Guards.

'Quick, behind the prison coach,' exclaimed Lord Lurkybert.

The Prime Minister's expression went from smug jubilance to horror as she realised, from recent experience, what was about to happen. She screeched at her Guards to move out of the way, but it was too late. With a series of booming sounds, a round of large black sticky missiles whistled through the air. As they hit the Guards, their metallic limbs juddered to a creaking stop as the thick gloopy mess they were covered in solidified.

'Idiots!' screamed the Prime Minister, becoming so enraged she managed to break an arm free from the tar encasing her and point up to the airship. 'I said shoot it down!' she shouted, as the cannon went off again.

After a few rounds had been fired and more of the Prime Minister's Guards had become entombed in the goo missiles, the cannon suddenly stopped. Arthur looked up to see his Aunt Eliza leaning out of the window with a very concerned expression on her face as the cannon shook with plumes of smoke coming out of it. She shrugged her shoulders at Arthur before disappearing back into the carriage.

'Now's your chance, destroy it!' said the Prime Minister.

'She's a sitting duck,' said Mr Quilymere, as more Guards marched along the bridge towards them.

'Not if I can help it,' growled Lord Lurkybert. 'Anyone for a game of skittles?' he said, looking at the prison coach.

Cragg jumped into action as it dawned on him what Lord Lurkybert was getting at. With all his strength, he pushed the coach up the bridge. As it built up speed, he let it go. The coach crashed straight through the oncoming Guards knocking some down and pushing others over the side of the bridge.

'STEEEE-RIKE!' cried out Lord Lurkybert, jumping in the air.

'No, no, nooo!' cried out the Prime Minister, fighting with her tarry tomb. A crack appeared in the solidified tar allowing her to free her other arm and a wing.

As one of the Guards went over the side of the bridge, it grabbed the coach pulling it over with it, leaving Cragg staring face to furnaced face with the remaining Guards.

'Hang on laddie, we're on our way!' cried Lord Lurkybert, seeing Cragg's predicament.

Mr Quilymere straightened his back and clenched his fists. 'If we go down, we go down fighting,' he said, running towards the Guards with Lord Lurkybert.

'The Society NEVER surrenders,' said Madam Plummwith, hitching up her dress and tucking it into the pair of breeches she was wearing underneath it, before following the others into battle.

Arthur watched on with great admiration as Aggie threw off her rags, rolled up her sleeves and charged at one of the Guards herself, sending it flying off the bridge and into the snowy abyss below. Jack was close behind as he too threw himself into battle.

If Aggie and Jack, two people of some advancing years, were willing to take on the Guards, thought Arthur, then so should he. Picking up a metal arm that was lying on the bridge, he brandished it like a club. As he hit a Guard over the head, sending it spinning, he caught a glimpse of Madam Plummwith. She was bounding about the bridge performing some very impressive acrobatics. Throwing her legs and arms around in a most deadly manner, she knocked the heads and limbs off any Guard unfortunate enough to get in her way.

Arthur and Cragg soon teamed up. Arthur jumped onto Cragg's shoulders and he swung the metal arm at any nearby Guards, knocking their heads off. Cragg grabbed at the Guards' arms and tore them off before he kicked what was left of them off the side of the bridge.

Just when Arthur thought they had defeated the Prime Minister's metallic army, a fresh wave of Guards appeared. An exhausted Arthur was not only horrified to see them, but he was equally dismayed to see what they were wheeling along the bridge.

'Look out!' shouted Mr Quilymere to Eliza, on seeing what the Guards had brought with them. The Guards stopped and quickly aimed the new, and even larger cannons, at the airship.

The Prime Minister laughed manically. 'I've told you already, you can't win,' she said, then pointed up at the airship. 'Destroy it!'

BOOM! BOOM! BOOM!

Arthur and The Society watched on helplessly as the Guards fired their cannons. As cannonballs flew through the air and towards the hot air balloon, Eliza calmly looked out through the carriage window as they hurtled towards her.

'Move out of the way!' shouted up Mr Quilymere.

Arthur couldn't watch so he turned away. When some moments had passed, and there didn't come the crashing sound he'd expected, he looked up. Arthur was both stunned and jubilant to see the airship was still in the air having taken no damage.

The Prime Minister screeched out in blind frustration. 'Shoot it down! Shoot it down, you fools!' she shrieked, twisting and managing to free her second wing.

More cannonballs were fired off at the airship and this time Arthur watched on curious to see what prevented the airship from taking any damage the first time. He was amazed at what he saw. Before the cannonballs hit the airship, they pinged off some kind of an invisible shield leaving the airship completely undamaged.

If the Prime Minister wasn't angry enough already, it didn't help matters that Eliza waved at her. 'Traitors!' the Prime Minister screeched, completely breaking free from the tar and taking to the air again where she faced the airship head on. Lightning arced across her whole body and began to form around her hands.

A foot suddenly appeared through the opening on the underside of the old train carriage and gave the cannon, suspended from it, a hearty kick. It spluttered and came back to life before it rotated around to face the Prime Minister. As the Prime Minister held up her hands in readiness to fire bolts of lightning at Eliza's ship, Mrs Boil appeared next to Eliza, her face smeared with grease, grasping a large wrench in one hand.

The Prime Minister let out a loud shriek. She was instantly shut up as an enormous ball of tar fired from the cannon, hit her before she could move out of the way and sent her plummeting to the ground below.

Arthur and the others cheered. As they looked up, a hatch in the bottom of the airship opened up and a rope ladder rolled down towards them. A familiar head peered over the side of the hole and smiled at everyone below. 'That shut her up, didn't it?' said Eliza, smiling down at them.

Before anyone could reply, a crack appeared down the lump of solidified tar encasing the Prime Minister. It widened before a long, bony hand burst through.

'Well, maybe not for long. Looks like we'll have to hold off on the chat. Quick, climb aboard, but be jolly careful, it's rather blustery!' said Eliza.

One by one, everyone climbed the rope ladder until there were only three of them left. 'Hurry, get on,' said Madam Plummwith to Aggie.

Aggie looked at Jack then back at Madam Plummwith. 'We're staying,' she said. 'We still have unfinished business to take care of.'

'But...' began Madam Plummwith.

'No buts, just go now!' said Jack, seeing the Prime Minister start to work her way out of the lump of tar.

Madam Plummwith saluted Aggie and Jack. 'It's been an honour,' she said, before climbing the ladder. On the way up, she shouted to Eliza, 'Jack and Aggie aren't coming with us. Can you give them some cover?'

Eliza nodded and aimed the cannon at the remaining Guards and fired off a fresh round of missiles. As the tar hit them, it gave the Corbeaus just enough time to escape. For two people who'd been imprisoned for as long as they had, Aggie and Jack made a surprisingly sprightly departure, hurrying along the bridge and vanishing into the blizzard.

As The Society members climbed aboard the airship, Ida gave each of them a hug. It was Mr Quilymere who had tears in his eyes. 'My dearest Ida, I felt sure we had lost you forever,' he said. He then turned to Eliza. 'I can't thank you enough,' he said to her.

Eliza grinned back. 'All part of the service, my good man,' she said, slapping him on the back.

Arthur ran over to his parents and hugged them for what seemed like forever. He had never felt more relieved to see them.

'I think you may have some explaining to do,' Arthur's mother said to him.

'I know, I can explain,' Arthur said.

'Yes, it's been a rather eventful few hours,' said his father, a grin spreading across his face. 'If only we could show you what we have just seen. You'd never believe it, son.'

Arthur looked curiously over at his mother and she smiled back. 'Oh Arthur, we've seen it!' she said.

'Seen what?' asked Arthur.

'The inside of The Storm, of course!' said Eliza, winking at him as she stood with her hands on her hips.

Arthur's mouth dropped open. 'No way!' he said.

'Impossible!' said Mr Hardgrave. 'This flimsy vessel would never survive.' He emphasised his point by gesturing to the roaring wall of wind just outside the back window.

'We've just seen them appear from it. What more proof do you need?' said Mr Quilymere. He then turned to Eliza, 'But, I am still quite at a loss as to how you accomplished it.'

Eliza began hoisting up the rope ladder, pulling on levers and turning dials. 'All down to the Electromagnetron, old boy,' she said.

'Electro whatty?' said Lord Lurkybert.

'Electromagnetron. It's the same thing that stopped those pathetic cannonballs from smashing my ship to pieces. It creates a shield around the ship, protecting it from being destroyed.'

There was one question Arthur wanted to ask but Madam Plummwith, who had been busily smoothing back down her dress, got in there first, 'What do we do now?'

Eliza stopped moving around and faced Madam Plummwith, 'We're off to The Other Lands, of course.' Before she could reply, Eliza had grabbed the ship's wheel and spun it on its spindle.

*

As the airship began to turn, the Prime Minister completely broke free from the solidified tar. As she looked up, she roared out in anger. Quickly, she glided over to one of the remaining cannons, picked it and brandished it like it were nothing more than a giant pistol. Without a moment's hesitation, she pointed it at Eliza's airship, took aim and fired. Unlike the other cannonballs, this one headed for the contraption poking out of the top of the balloon, the one object the Prime Minister felt sure was protecting the ship from being hit.

Just before the airship disappeared into The Storm, the cannonball clipped it. As a great shower of sparks and smoke billowed from the metal rod like device, the Prime Minister looked on grinning to herself.

# CHAPTER 33

## *Inside The Storm*

'Ladies and gentlemen, please grab yourself a seat and buckle up. We're going in,' said Eliza, pulling down her smoky goggles. She turned a few dials, pulled on a lever then gripped tightly to the ship's wheel.

Nobody needed to be told twice because no sooner had Eliza said this, the carriage began to violently shake. 'Please, tell me that this is normal?' shouted Mr Quilymere over the noise, clutching tightly onto his seat.

Eliza looked over her shoulder. 'Absolutely, my dear fellow!' she said. 'Nothing to worry yourself about.' As the airship moved forward, there suddenly came a loud bang outside and Eliza jumped. 'Okay, possibly that,' she said quietly to herself, pulling up her goggles and glancing across at the brass dials on the panel beside her.

'What was that?' demanded an alarmed Madam Plummwith.

'Nothing to worry yourself about, Eudora,' said Eliza, peering at the dial with 'shield' written below it that now had its needle sat in the red zone.

'That didn't sound like nothing to me,' said Mr Quilymere.

'It's just the shield. It's being a bit temperamental, that's all.'

'The shield?' said Mr Hardgrave. 'You're not seriously telling us that the only thing from preventing this ship from being torn apart isn't working?'

'Like I say, nothing to worry yourself about, old chap. I'm pretty sure that we'll be fine.'

'Pretty sure?' said Mr Hardgrave. 'For the love of all that's good and gracious, we're all going to die.'

As if on cue, the airship lurched sideways and a bell started ringing. 'Ignore that,' said Eliza, but Arthur wasn't sure that he could.

Eliza then banged the shield dial with her fist, making it stop. 'There! See, fixed.' The dial hand rotated out of the red but only by a small amount.

As Eliza's passengers' terrified faces looked out through the windows, and they gripped tightly to their seats, they could see that they were now inside The Storm itself. The airship shook as bright flashes of light exploded outside. As Arthur looked out of the window, he was horrified to see great mountainous clumps of rock and earth begin to bounce off the shield.

'What's happening?' said Madam Plummwith.

'Just what we need, Storm debris,' shouted Eliza over her shoulder as she wrestled with the ship's wheel. 'Nothing to worry about.'

'I wish she'd stop saying that,' said Mr Boil.

The ferocity of the wind was unrelenting as it screamed and roared around the carriage. Arthur looked over at the dial and willed it not to go into the red again, but he wasn't at all hopeful. If any more bits of debris hit the carriage, Arthur thought, then that would be it. They'd be smashed into a million pieces.

If matters weren't already bleak enough, a flash of lightning suddenly illuminated the great expanse around them to reveal an enormous silhouetted shape. Eliza groaned. 'Hang on everyone. We have company,' she said.

Arthur could scarcely believe what he was seeing. Sailing on the wind, as if it were the Great River of Londonian, was a gigantic wooden ship. As it moved towards them, Arthur could see that its body was made from the parts of many other ships, all bolted together haphazardly. Its great distressed sails pulled taut against their masts. As it grew closer, there came a series of thunderous booms.

'Hang on!' shouted Eliza over the roar of The Storm as she spun the ship's wheel. Moments later, and with a series of bright flashes, a number of cannonballs bounced off the shield making Arthur jump. Eliza looked at the shield dial as its needle hung just above the red zone. 'She won't take many more hits like that I'm afraid,' Eliza said.

Mr Boil was now sucking his thumb, rocking back and forth.

'Who are they?' shouted Mr Quilymere.

Eliza spun the wheel from side to side, somehow managing to steer the airship out of the way of the next round of missiles. 'Pirates,' she shouted back. 'Well, I think they are. They're not friendly, that's for sure!'

'What do they want from us?' asked Madam Plummwith.

'I don't know. I've never stayed around long enough to ask.'

A great bolt of lightning cut across the sky. As it did so, it illuminated the ship again and, this time, Arthur got a sense of how big it was. Across its side, many portholes had opened up and from them, there were countless cannons all pointing at the airship. 'Eliza, I insist you get us out of here, now!' said Madam Plummwith.

'I couldn't agree with you more, old girl,' replied Eliza, spinning the ship's wheel. As the ship started to turn around, another series of cannonballs fired off.

An alarm began to ring as the needle rolled around back into the red. 'Ignore that,' said Eliza.

There came a great crashing sound as a couple of cannonballs finally broke through the shield and smashed into the side of the carriage. Arthur and the others cried out in shock as the ship shook wildly and the force of the wind blew inside the ship.

'We're all going to die,' whimpered Mr Hardgrave again, clinging tightly to his seat. 'So much for the rescue mission.'

The pirate ship had moved close enough for Arthur to see the baying crew of unsavoury characters aboard it. They looked more like ghosts than people. All were bearded and deathly pale, their

mean sunken eyes blazing with a cruelty and ferocity usually reserved for the insane. They aimed their cannons at the ship again and began firing. The shield was now so weak, it barely managed to stop the onslaught. Bits of the ship were now breaking off in a shower of splinters and sparks. It was obvious to Arthur that his Aunt Eliza's ship wouldn't take much more punishment before it was completely destroyed.

'Get us out of here!' shouted Mr Quilymere.

'Working on it!' shouted back Eliza, pulling on a big brass handle beside her.

The ship dropped like a stone. Arthur and the others onboard shrieked out as they left their seats, only to be kept from hitting the ceiling by the belts around their waists. Eliza, clinging tightly to the ship's wheel with one hand, pushed another handle and the airship flew underneath the pirate ship. Even over the sound of The Storm, Arthur heard the pirates roar out in anger.

Ahead, Arthur saw a bright light that appeared out from the gloom.

'Ha! There she is. The other side of The Storm,' shouted Eliza, pointing at it, grinning. The pirate ship above them hadn't given up yet. It aimed its cannons down at the airship and continued to fire at them.

Another bell started ringing. 'Now what,' growled Eliza. The dial with 'Altitude' written beneath it had its needle planted firmly in the red zone too. 'Ignore it,' she said.

Eliza pulled on another brass handle and the carriage began to sharply rise again, pushing Arthur back into his seat. The light grew brighter until, with a shower of sparks, the airship burst through The Storm wall.

The light was so bright it blinded Arthur. For a moment, all that he could see was whiteness. He could still hear perfectly well, and what he heard next was his Aunt Eliza shouting out, 'Hold on!'.

As his eyes refocused, Arthur saw that they had broken through The Storm wall and the airship was crashing its way through some very tall and extremely dense trees. As they hurtled through the branches, it was accompanied by some very worrying tearing sounds and then an extremely loud hissing noise of escaping air. They all held on for dear life as they watched the trees whip past the broken windows. Eliza was still grasping hold of the ship's wheel as Arthur gripped his chair's arms and braced himself for impact.

With a final long ripping sound, the balloon was torn free from the carriage. 'That's not good,' said Eliza, looking behind her to see the balloon hanging from some branches.

With nothing to keep them in the air, the carriage hurtled towards the ground. Arthur had no time to think about dying as the carriage suddenly burst through the canopy, and like a giant wooden skipping stone, it hit a river before it bounced back off it again. The carriage sailed through the air for a few brief moments before it came down and hit the water again. This time it didn't bounce, instead it produced a great tidal wave of water as it came to a sudden and abrupt stop.

Before it had a chance to start sinking, Eliza got back to her feet and pulled on another lever. Out of the sides of the carriage, two great balloons inflated. It was only then that she collapsed to the floor, completely and utterly, exhausted. After all the chaos and confusion, an eerie silence filled the carriage. 'Is everybody all right?' Eliza asked. There came back muttered sounds of yes as the carriage bobbed gently up and down on the water.

It was Arthur who first got to his feet and made his way over to the front window. As he reached it and looked outside, he was lost for words. He continued to stare for what seemed like an eternity, not being able to take his eyes off of the view in front of him. It was only when his Aunt Eliza finally stood behind him and put her hands on his shoulders that he even blinked. 'Where are we?' he asked.

'Haven't you worked it out for yourself yet, Arty?' she said, smiling down at him.

Arthur looked back outside again with an expression of pure wonder and excitement. 'Are we?' he asked.

'Yes, we are indeed!' replied Eliza. 'Welcome, Arthur, to The Other Lands.'

To be continued…

LONDONIAN

# ABOUT THE AUTHOR

**Mike Oakley** is an artist and writer. For over twenty-five years, he has created artwork for many award-winning video games and virtual reality experiences. By night though, he loves nothing more than to write highly imaginative novels for both children and adults alike. Mike grew up, and now lives, in the South of England with his wife and two daughters. '*The Society of Incredible Stories*' is, in his own words, the greatest creative achievement of his life.

# ABOUT THE ILLUSTRATOR

**Andy Oakley** has been a professional artist for over twenty-five years. In that time, he has worked in the video games industry, having been associated with many well respected, and BAFTA winning, games. Now, he has also lent his amazing artistic skills to '*The Society of Incredible Stories*' where he has created over 80 illustrations for the first book alone. Andy lives in the South of England with his wife and three children.

Visit us at

# www.dormouse-publishing.com

to keep up to date on all the latest Society news, competitions and
to sign up to our newsletter.

If you have enjoyed reading this book, we would love
you to leave a review through the 'Contact Us' page on
our website or on Amazon.

(Kids, please get permission from an adult first)

Printed in Great Britain
by Amazon